NEW PLAINS REVIEW

New Plains Review

New Plains Review is edited by students and faculty of the English Department in the College of Liberal Arts at the University of Central Oklahoma. The political, social, or artistic commentary represents the views of the writers and artists, and inclusion in the journal does not indicate editorial endorsement or non-endorsement.

New Plains Review does not claim to represent the views of the University of Central Oklahoma.

The image above is from a painting titled **Phantom Warriors** by acclaimed Native American artist and UCO alumnus Sherman Chaddlesone (Kiowa).

newplainsreview@submittable.com

Copyright © 2025 by New Plains Review Student Publishing
All rights reserved. No part of this book may be reproduced in any manner whatsoever without written permission except in the case of brief quotations embodied in critical articles and reviews.
First Printing, 2025

Masthead

Executive Editor & Production Designer - Shay Rahm

Senior Editors

Caitlin Yates
Capri Burton
CJ Grammer
Grant Zehrung
Hannah Lobaugh

Assistant Editors

Axel Sanchez
Bryan Raines
Drew Thompson
Estela Aida Castillo Melia
Hannah Wilkerson
Jenny Nelson
Jessica Jones
Ky Nealy
Madilyn Green
Sydney Harris
Trevor Wallar

Cover Artist - M Russek

Contents

V	Masthead
1	Cover Art – M. Russek
3	Xanax Diaries – Daniel Lewis
9	Hammerly – Lindsey Warren
11	Degrees – Lindsey Warren
13	Your Goldsharp Eye – Lindsey Warren
15	The Thief of Joy – Lily Horn
19	Après Divorce – Alan Hill
21	Swing Shift – Anthony Chatfield
27	To Quoin the Term – CS Crowe
29	Roadside Crew – Maureen Sherbondy
35	I Miss Trees – Matthew Wallace
37	Headless – Alena Graedon
45	Mother Wolf – Savannah Brooks
53	Caribbean Blue – Sara Shea

57	Reflections From... – Sara Shea
59	Swamp Lily – Sara Shea
63	The Psychopomp – Elizabeth Rae Bullmer
65	Do We Inherit the Way We Die? – Elizabeth Rae Bullmer
67	Please Define the Word Legacy – Elizabeth Rae Bullmer
69	Ophelia: A Christmas Special – ZiXuan Angel Xin
89	Visual Art – Robin Young
95	Cosmic – E. A. McCarthey
97	Bear Cave – E. A. McCarthey
100	Carnelian – E. A. McCarthey
103	Self – John Pring
105	Anaphora as a Dying Son – John Pring
107	Coffee Date – Colton Johnson
117	Bedtime – Michael J. Galko
119	The Crazy Card is an Eleven of Hearts – Michael J. Galko
121	The One Hundred and First Tale – Michael J. Galko
125	Real American Lover – Jacie Eubanks
129	The Hermaphroditic Seed – Jacie Eubanks
133	Inspector #1 – John Delaney

135   Adopting a Cat: Checklist – John Delany

137   What We Lose – Rowan Waller

139   Secrets Our Bodies Keep – Colleen S. Harris

141   Visual Art – Cynthia Yatchman

147   Desolation – Lindsay Thurman

155   The Pool Party – Joylyn Chai

169   About the Contributors

Cover Art

M. Russek

The Leaf Between Worlds

1
Xanax Diaries

Daniel Lewis

"Now you still like working at Bone and Joint?"
Grandma Rita smiled,
a fragile voice wisping
from beneath glazed-over innocence.

...the fifth time she had asked this question in a broken twenty minutes.

I never minded this though.
Too sweet and thoughtful a person to ever get frustrated with,
at least that's what I'd always thought of her my whole life:

The kind of person you couldn't help but be fond of
because she always remembered your name. And she didn't just
remember your name, she remembered every annoying, cumbersome detail about your life
you somehow felt comfortable dumping on her.
She even remembered things you didn't tell her. She could recall the day,
month, and year she met you,
what you were wearing, what kind of mood you were in,
how honest of a person you were.

Cruel irony is seeing someone once so incredibly sharp
so pathetically degraded.

My Aunt Carrie would yell harshly back at Grandma Rita in an overly annoyed tone,
a small, cigarette-worn frame flipping crisped quesadillas for the three of us,
as if this would repay Grandma for taking her in,
for not letting meth and alcohol leave her homeless.

When she moved in, Grandma was already slipping away, a victim of her own
chemical demon...

piles of groceries in her kitchen she would keep buying multiple times because she forgot she
already had,
stacks of shut-off notices from not remembering to pay the bills,
laundry caked over with mildew she'd left in her washer.
She had even gotten lost for hours a couple times while driving,
calling my dad in tears to come pick her up.

At least with Carrie there, we didn't have to send her to a nursing home.

"I *do* miss the hospital sometimes."
I smiled back at Grandma.
"That's nice!"
She rocked back in her blue recliner, beaming at me fondly.
No point trying to remind Grandma
that Bone and Joint Hospital was four jobs ago.

She would ask about it again within minutes regardless of what I told her.

In just a few unforgivingly short months, our words
would be rendered unintelligible to her completely.
    Even her own words became foreign to her.
        She would look urgently into my eyes, her gaze swimming
            right and left, searching for the database of vocabulary
                      that used to be so familiar to her.
                            Her ache to speak palpable,
                but the sentence she toiled to construct would never surface
                      beyond a few nonsensical syllables.
                            It wasn't long before she
                              quit speaking at all.

                                    Her Xanax,
                        her precious safespace. Withered her,
                              eaten her hollow…

          The way a mind falls apart is an interesting thing.
          It sheds itself in layers, pulling to pieces softly overtime.
              It is the gradual opening of a cursed flower,
              one whose exposed center does not give life,
                        but death.

The formation and use of human language depends on memory.
The development of language in childhood is correlated almost perfectly with
the development of memory.
As we become ourselves, as our pool of experience fills,
so does our prowess in communicating our ideas,
our feelings, who we are.

                You cannot learn or use language without memory.

                Yet I would watch Grandma Rita try helplessly to do just this,
                    to put her thoughts into words she no longer remembered.
    Her hippocampi, in conjunction with the posterior regions of her left temporal lobe,
             would have normally retrieved these words effortlessly for her.
                  But these pathways were now corroded, decayed,
                      unkempt trails in the forest of her brain,
            neural routes eaten away by a lifetime of pharmaceutical solace.
            (doctor-prescribed, of course)

Grandma's condition eventually worsened to a point where it was no longer
                      "medically advisable"
to keep giving her Xanax, or any of the various opioids she'd grown to depend on.
                The poison chalice, finally lifted from her.

...but only after it had stolen everything she loved,
only after it became the sole comfort she had left in this world.
She only got worse after that.

I remember seeing her cry, writhe, haunted
by pain and a crippling panic she'd lost the ability
to name or numb herself to.
Would it have been kinder to let her drugs of choice finish her off?
Should we have granted her that mercy?

Entering Grandma Rita's house was once a thing of joy.
her laugh of a "hello" seemed to hug you
just before her arms did the same.
There were always a million cats there too,
perched throughout her collection of bunny figurines,
drawn in from the streets by her warmth.

I fed her a small pinch of a weed gummy one time,
desperate to give her even a shade of the relief
her pills once had.
But it soon became apparent that the first time a person gets stoned
should not be after they have advanced dementia.

"Oh yeah. I'm sure she'll be fine!"
Carrie encouraged me after I looked up any possible interactions
with the cholinesterase inhibitors and glutamate regulators she was now on,
our family's feeble attempt to keep as much of Grandma Rita as we could.

I put the sliver of gummy on her tongue and she smiled,
pleasantly caught off guard by her favorite flavor,
black cherry. She chewed it unquestioningly.

Normally in those days, Grandma spent almost all her time sitting,
all but catatonic, her blue recliner turned to face the giant TV.
She would still reflexively open her mouth to spoonfuls of food,
and could still take short, zombified walks around the yard or the mall
when we took her by the arm and lugged her around.
But unprompted, she would sit endlessly,
in and out of sleep, motionless apart from her bouts of pain and panic:
no goals, no desires, no memories...
She wore a diaper, no longer remembering to respond to
even the most basic of her body's urges.

So, it was strange when an hour and a half after giving Grandma the gummy,
Carrie and I noticed her blue recliner was empty.

"AAAAAAAAAHHH!"

Grandma Rita's voice suddenly cried out from down the hall.
The muffled echo gave away that she must be in the bathroom.
Carrie and I busted into the small, pink-tiled room to find Grandma
sitting on the floor in front of the toilet with her pants down.
She was crying, shaking, terrified beyond reason,
her eyes bloodshot.

"Come on, Mom, let's go back to the living room,"
Carrie grunted as she grabbed Grandma under the shoulder to hoist her up.

"NOOOOO! SSSSSTOP!"

Grandma belted up at Carrie in fear.

...her own daughter a complete stranger to her.

Carrie let go, staring back at her in wide-eyed shock.
We both looked at Grandma and then each other, unsure
if this brief breaking of her vocal silence was a miracle,
or a glitch in her grey matter matrix:
a transient, cannabinoid-revived hiccup of processing
in the shriveled synapses still linking the Wernicke's area and Broca's area
of her left-brain hemisphere to her left hippocampus.

Grandma cried and wailed harder as we got her to her feet.
Once she was back in her recliner, she continued to suffer
from the absolute worst of her panic attacks either of us had ever seen.

After shaking, sweating, screaming,
and trying to get up again for almost three more hours,
she passed out for the remainder of the day and night,
my ill-conceived attempt to give her any relief an utter failure.

Those were some of the last steps Grandma would ever take in her life,
and the last words she would ever speak...

That blue recliner.
Many of my 12-year-old weekends were spent there
watching cartoons while she made me pancakes,
for every meal if I wanted.
"Don't tell your mom!" she would snicker
as she plopped down next to me in the cozy chair.

It was hard to tell how much of Grandma was
still trapped inside this deflated statue of herself.

What kinds of thoughts could she possibly still have,
in a mindscape unarticulated by memory or language?
Was she now something primal, animalistic, the raw instincts
of our beginnings on some African plain?
Had she retreated into the *Jungian* core of personality,
lost to the mythological archetypes that ruled the collective unconscious?
Or had her soul already left this world?
How much of Rita still colored her mental rumblings?

And this snowballing lifelessness didn't just afflict her brain.
Xanax and the other drugs
had soured many of her other organs as well.
Grandma Rita soon died in a hospital bed, poked full of plastic tubes and wires.
Her body lay there, diminished, reduced to nothing more than another sob story of
modern ~~addiction~~ medicine.

It was hard to accept such a pointless end to her tale.
Perhaps she finally met the God she used to pray to.
Or were the never-ending prescriptions Grandma relied on her whole life
a devil's contract signed in blood?
Had the devil come to collect his due?

Even this would be less chilling an ending than

the cold meaninglessness of her final chapter…

After letting me dig the grave
with my little plastic shovel,
Grandma padded my tears away and smiled,
"Now don't you worry about Missy."
She wrapped my favorite cat
in a yellow blanket
and placed her in the soft ground.
"She isn't hurting anymore."

2

Hammerly

Lindsey Warren

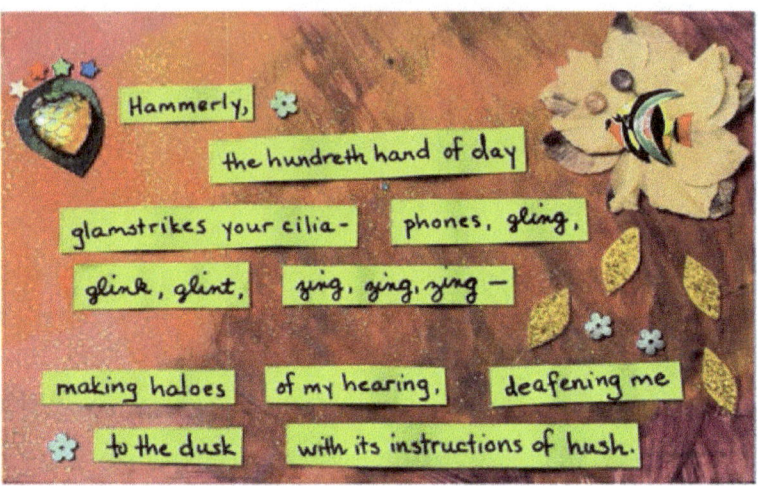

3
Degrees

Lindsey Warren

Degrees dressed auroric, amberchecked, assured, ceaseless from your skin. When I come through the turned-off starcaps and into the genius of your hands, I burn nucleus over all blended horizons.

4

Your Goldsharp Eye

Lindsey Warren

5

The Thief of Joy

Lily Horn

The beige walls of my room are littered with boards filled with a kaleidoscope of words.

Words written by people I will never meet, that somehow found their way into my mind and lobotomized the thoughts that stick like glue to the crevices of my brain.

Picture-perfect words, encapsulating all of the thoughts that I could never write myself.

At a loss for words to describe the emotions ravaging the brain that is anything but kind to me.

Each day, I hang up a new board, praying that maybe this one will be the soundboard that finally blocks out all the noise that deafens my mind.

I put up more and more of these boards, hoping for a positive result, while all it does is serve as a depressing reminder that, no matter how hard I try, I always fall short of my peers.

Never as good with my words as the mouths I see moving every day.

As I start my second lap, someone else has already crossed the finish line, and they have the gold medal hanging around their throat.

Their eyes glisten with pride, intoxicated with the putrid smell of their own words.

They paint the most convoluted murals with their words, while I cannot even finish a paint-by-number with mine.

They articulate their thoughts so well, crafted with the most vibrant language, while all of my words seem to be a different shade of beige; are my thoughts that dull too?

How do they do it so well, but I cannot?

Am I even doing the right thing with my life?

I look nothing like the people around me, sound nothing like them, write nothing like them.

They tell me this is a good thing, that having your own voice is what distinguishes you as a writer, but this always feels like a bandage they slap over the wound I self-inflict, trying to stop my words from oozing out.

If they tell me what they think I want to hear, maybe I'll stop talking, maybe I'll stop writing, maybe I'll stop trying so hard.

Are my words as put together and as pretty as theirs?

Their words look like a gift that was wrapped at a store when they bought it, complete with a big red bow, while mine was thrown into whatever bag I found in the back of my closet, topped with random tissue paper I found crammed in a drawer that does not even match my bag.

What used to be an escape for me is now just a breeding ground for comparison and disappointment.

If only I could write my way out of my feelings like I write my way into them.

6

Après Divorce

Alan Hill

I have stored in the wheel well of long-distance jet.

If I drop, I will die.

If I stay, clutch a little longer, I will also die.

I know it.

It is time to let go, enjoy my body as it
moves through air
for once, stop thinking, allow myself to be
overwhelmed
prisoner of my senses, to
take that little time as my own
before I hit the ground; as we all must.

Let me hold a second longer to this thin inhuman life
say goodbye to my son, daughter, pets
before my fingers come away

I fall backwards into who I must be, if I am to live.

7

Swing Shift

Anthony Chatfield

"Exacerbate…"

"Excuse me?!"

Theo looks up to see the barista's horrified expression, eyes wide, mouth pursed. She could be a TV pundit after the State of the Union—puffed up and pilloried by the 'moral depravity' of *the other guys*. And like a pundit, she completely misunderstood.

"Apologies. I was just thinking of a word. Exacerbate. *To make a problem worse*."

"Uh huh…" Andrea, Theo is pretty sure her name is Andrea, sketches his drink order on the side of a cup. She gestures to the end of the bar and shifts her attention to the guy behind him.

"Maybe aggravate is better…" Theo murmurs as he shuffles past the sputtering espresso machine.

* * *

Barnaby Willoughby nods, a slight tilt to his chin, and winks at the barista, he's pretty sure her name is Annette. "You, my dear, are…so wonderful every morning. Does anyone ever tell you that?" Barnaby, who will not stand to be called Barney by anyone except possibly his mother, but only on Mother's Day and Christmas Eve, coos.

"No, never," She says flatly, a blue Sharpie pressing roughly against the side of the polyethylene-lined cup. It squeaks sharply as she pushes.

"Oh, well you are, my dear." Barnaby pushes a lock of hair away from his eyes and coughs uncomfortably, leans forward a bit, starts to wink and then pulls his phone out of his pocket.

"That it?"

"Yes, thank you. For now, at least. Much to be done today. Much to be done."

"End of the bar." She gestures to her right.

* * *

"Those guys bothering you?" Camilla steps to the counter and adjusts her glasses. She shuffles the slab of aluminum that is her laptop from one elbow crook to the other. "I saw they were bothering you." She answers for, what was her name again, the barista? Alex?

"No, not really," Alex responds, holding her Sharpie aloft, toward Camilla. "What can I get you?"

"Oh, well, I'd love something cheerful and energizing. I am absolutely loaded with ideas this morning. So many ideas." Camilla smiles brightly, but Alex simply stares.

"Cold brew?"

"Yes, that would be splendid. Splash of cream."

"End of the bar."

"Ah, yes, of course." Camilla passes her a ten-dollar bill and smiles widely.

* * *

It's not aggravate...or exacerbate. Theo takes a sip of his drink, dark roast, no cream or sugar, just nutty, acidic caffeine. Straight to his veins. Simple and effective. Except this morning. What is the damn word he's trying to think of? He taps absently at the keyboard, a cursor blinking again, again, again on the blank white screen. What is the damn word?

* * *

Barnaby smiles at Annette, but she isn't looking, too busy with another customer. He sips at his drink, a caramel macchiato with three pumps of vanilla creme and four shots of espresso, one shot of decaf espresso. He licks his lips and watches as she presses the Sharpie into the same divot on the same size of cup that he is now drinking out of. Is he jealous? Is that a thing? He should be writing. He sets the cup down and sees that she's written *Barney* in wide looping script across the top of the cup.

* * *

Camilla taps gently at her keyboard. It jiggles against the edge of the table. She can't use the keyboard on the laptop. It hurts her wrist, but a full-sized keyboard doesn't fit on these tiny round coffee shop tables, so she's using a smaller, compact keyboard with a bit of an incline to it. It works, but it jiggles. She decides this exact detail would make a wonderful story. Opening a new tab, she starts jotting down details. *Tired barista. Jiggling keyboard. Coffee shop.* Perfect, a plan for tomorrow.

* * *

Agitate? Vex? Antagonize? No. No. No. None of these are right. Too aggressive. Too pretentious. Too solitary. Theo needs a word that speaks to a room full of people. To everyone feeling a collective sense of agita. Of unending anxiety. An itch that can't be scratched. And then…someone makes it worse. What is the word for that? The cursor blinks, and he realizes his cup is empty.

* * *

Annette is on break now. Barnaby sees her outside smoking a cigarette. Nasty habit, smoking. Barnaby tried it once on a sojourn to France. Seemed appropriate. Everyone smokes in France. Well not everyone, but anyone worth talking to. It's romantic. He decides he doesn't mind Annette smoking. The way she gently rolls the cigarette around her lips, arms crossed, apron pooled around her waist. He wonders if she has an extra cigarette he could borrow. He scratches a couple of quick lines in a jet-black Moleskine notebook, pockets it and the pencil, and makes for the door.

* * *

Tap, tap, tap. The table shakes incessantly, and Camilla wonders if there might be another one in the coffee shop that isn't so loose.

She looks for a barista and doesn't find one. So, instead pulls a napkin from beneath her keyboard and folds it three times, stuffing it under the offending leg. A burst of inspiration rushes through her. *A college student. Stuck in a coffee shop. Left to her own devices, with nothing but napkins and empty cups.*

* * *

"You still here?" Louis raises an eyebrow as he drops his backpack in the corner and pulls an apron out of the cubby behind the espresso machine.

"Nancy called in sick."

"Suuure. Sick. Saw her last night around Pioneer Square. She's zero-point-two sick. Got a case of that tequila flu, if you know what I mean."

Angela smiles and nods. "Sure, Louis. I know what you mean."

"How's the crowd today?"

"As full of bullshit as ever."

"That bad?"

"Nah, but that one," Angela points to a middle-aged man in a faded blazer, hair combed loosely over a growing bald spot, "keeps attempting to hit on me."

"Attempting?"

"Yeah, he hasn't actually gotten up the nerve to be full-on creepy yet, but he's trying."

"Maybe it's research?"

Angela laughs, tosses her apron on the dirty pile behind the counter, and raises an eyebrow. "If any of these weirdos ever publish something, I'll work your shifts for free for a month."

Louis starts to open his mouth, a knee-jerk response to the offer of free labor, but thinks better of himself.

"That's what I thought." She starts toward the door.

Camilla smiles and waves at her from her perch at the back of the shop. She's holding a handful of carefully folded napkins. "See you tomorrow, Alex!"

The perfectionist, Theo, exclaims without looking up: "Nettle!"

Barnaby looks up and smiles lasciviously but then seems to remember something and looks all around him as if someone will save him from the decision he just made.

Angela sighs and slips out the door. Yup, tomorrow. And the next day, and the day after that.

8

To Quoin the Term

CS Crowe

I learned we live inside the Patriarchy,
Because our lives are divided into four years wandering the wilderness,
Even though Jesus was born only eighty mothers before us,
And agriculture was invented only four hundred mothers before Him.

Do you understand how little divides us?
Even time can be measured with the dented tin cups and spoons
Passed down from your grandmother's kitchen.

We rip up carpet and linoleum and find wood and stone:
How many families and their mothers walked these halls?

We rip up keystones and foundations and find soil and loam:
How many songbirds and wildflowers called this home?

While our mothers built our homes from thread and butter,
Our fathers carried an axe into the wilderness
To level the earth while it was still soft for want of us.

If we worked together, you and I, it would only take us a day
To rip up the floorboards and tear down the foundation,
Imagine how much we could achieve in four years,
Imagine how much more we could achieve in a generation.

9

Roadside Crew

Maureen Sherbondy

Wilbur Crew had been removing animal carcasses from roads since he was ten years old, so when his son Johnny turned ten, he took him to work despite protests from his wife. As Wilbur packed up his large pickup truck with gloves, disposal bags, and other accouterments needed to perform the task, his wife Martha followed him up the long dirt driveway.

She muttered, "Boy's too young to see death, those poor creatures all bloodied and mangled."

"Nonsense," Wilbur added, "he's already a sissy. Time to make a man out of him."

"He's just sensitive, is all," Martha said, wiping photograph developing chemicals from her fingers onto a rag.

"Well, I started at his age and never once had one single nightmare. Boy will be fine." Wilbur rubbed Johnny's thick, dark hair. His entire hand was larger than his son's head.

Johnny looked up at his giant father, whose face was partially blocked by a hanging tree branch. It almost seemed as if he was part of that oak. Solid and impenetrable. The boy wanted to be cool like his father, the way he swaggered into a room. His father was the kind of man who commanded attention from farmers and townspeople in their small community.

In the evenings, Johnny would sit beside his father on the front porch, watching him blow perfect smoke rings into the night air. Not much of a talker, his father seemed like a person constantly deep in thought, much like his 5th-grade math teacher. And there was a scent that followed him, something rancid oozed from his pores. Maybe this was why his father never hugged anyone. Only the flies seemed to be drawn to the stink; they hovered around his large torso.

His mother, in comparison, was petite and chatty. Unlike his distant father, Johnny's mother hugged him often and read fantasy books aloud at night while running her hands through his hair, the same color as her own. She smelled like vanilla and sunshine.

After the pickup pulled away, Johnny pictured his mother returning to the darkroom to develop photos of farm silos, flowers, and birds. The same darkroom built by Wilbur Crew as a wedding gift twelve years earlier. When his mother was upstairs perfecting her art, or folding laundry, his father would refer to her as a nagging wife, which disturbed Johnny, but he was too fearful of his father to ever defy him. Sometimes when his father's voice grew too loud, Johnny's hands would tremble.

As the red pickup coasted down the two-lane highway, Johnny felt both proud to be going to work with his father, but also wishing he could one day take photos and learn how to make images appear that had never existed before. He realized, as the scenery shifted from land and farms to close-together houses and businesses, that he had no idea what his father actually did at work. Sure, he knew animal removal from busy roads was involved, but Johnny figured the creatures had died a natural death. His friend Steven, who had recently lost his grandpa, said his grandpa just fell asleep. At recess, they stopped trading Magic cards for a moment when Steven uttered the word *dead*. Johnny watched a black bird perch on the monkey bars and tried to figure out what this word actually looked like. Would that bird just drop from the air and fall asleep? The idea of death made the grandpa's passing sound peaceful and pleasant.

Fall mating season in North Carolina was a busy time for carcass removal. That's why Roadside Crew collected its biggest paycheck in October and November. Johnny's grandpa, who had started the business, had set up an ongoing contract with two counties. These contracts, along with other private jobs, kept food on the table and a roof over their head.

Friday night after students from college towns hit the highways, partying late and then driving on curvy roads, the carcass fallout was predictably high. As they cruised along on these same roads, Johnny's father played tunes from a local country radio station, but he turned the music off when spotting something off the shoulder. Johnny had worn blue jeans and a black shirt just like his father. He watched the scenery as the pickup slowed down, then parked in dirt near a forest of pine trees. Johnny adjusted his glasses to make out what his father pointed to.

Grabbing gloves and a mask, his father handed these items through the passenger window to Johnny. Then he opened the passenger door, and said, "You put these on. Stand beside me and just watch what I do for this first one."

Though his father didn't don a mask, he did slide on gloves. Johnny adjusted his own gloves, then spotted the large deer. He backed away nearly into the path of a passing car.

"Stay away from the road!" His father jerked him hard by the arm. Two vultures flew up from the road, their wings startling Johnny.

Rubbing his sore arm, he backed up into the forest, viewing the tan creature from there. The deer was bloody and damaged. Not the peaceful, sleeping animal he'd expected. Parts of its torso were missing, as if the vultures had carved some food out for breakfast. The deer's black eyes were open, yet empty of life. They reminded Johnny of two black marbles. Shiny and wet.

"Vultures got a meal," his father said. "Come on over here. Take a good look. Only way to get used to it."

Johnny was now clinging to a thin pine tree. Tears streamed down his cheeks. His father peeled his son's hands off the tree, then lifted him up. Together, they sat in the dirt inches from the creature.

Johnny closed his eyes. "I don't want to see it."

"Just open one eye."

"People get eaten up when they die?" Tires rushed by. The sound of wind grazed his ears.

His father's voice grew soft. "No. You go in a coffin in the ground. Besides, you don't feel anything when you die."

Johnny opened his eyes and looked from the deer's twisted neck to his father's eyes. His dark eyes had softened. Was he thinking of his own father's death? Johnny had never met his grandfather but had heard wild stories about the man.

Johnny noticed that the animal was bigger than his body. He couldn't help but imagine his own legs and torso and neck sprawled out on the road. Why wasn't his father upset about finding these dead animals on the road?

"How do you know what it feels like to die?"

"I just do."

Johnny said, "It's such a pretty animal. Why aren't you sad?"

"Look. It's part of life. Animals die. And we can't just leave them here. They rot and stink and cause a hazard. We have nothing to do with their death. We're like the garbage men for animals."

Johnny didn't like that his father was comparing this beautiful deer to plastic and cartons and cans that were set out on Mondays at the end of the dirt driveway. There was something cold about that. "Have you ever hit an animal?"

"Let's focus on the job. We have a whole day ahead of us. It's just hard the first time. It will get easier. That's what my father told me."

"But I don't want to do this. I don't want it to get easier. Is that why you don't talk much? Is that what you're always thinking about?"

His father bit his lip. "Kid, you question too much. Just like your mother."

"Maybe I can stay in the truck."

His father nodded.

***

Johnny had nightmares. In dreams, that dead deer stood up with a hole in its torso, then two marble eyes rolled out and landed in Johnny's pockets. He woke sweating and crying. The next time his father tried to bring him along to work, Johnny's mother stood with crossed arms, and shaking her head no.

"You're gonna turn that kid into a sissy, Martha!"

"And you're going to sleep on that lumpy couch again if you keep this up," his mother yelled back.

One day, when Johnny's mother was rocking on the porch chatting on the phone with her sister in South Carolina, Johnny took her camera. It was Veteran's Day and there was no school. He wandered near the road in search of something interesting to shoot. When he came across a dead possum, he viewed it from behind the lens. It seemed less frightening this way. He clicked and clicked as he'd seen his mother do on many occasions. Then he moved around and figured out where the sun was hitting so the angle of light wouldn't ruin the photo, another thing he'd heard his mother mention. By the end of the day, he'd snapped ten photos of that dead possum. Then he carefully returned the camera to its spot on his mother's dresser.

A month later, his father took him out again. This time he helped drag a baby fawn, three large deer carcasses, and several other creatures into the truck. It was easy to lift their weight because his father just pressed a button on his vehicle and the bed lowered to the ground. Together, they rolled the carcasses up into the bed.

At home, they washed the stink of death from their hands and arms. His father patted him on the back.

"Good job, boy. Here's some money for your labor."

Johnny took the ten dollar bill and stared at Alexander Hamilton. If he kept helping his father, he could buy a camera of his own. Maybe his father would stop calling him a sissy.

His mother had found the photos of the dead possum and hung the developed images in her dark room. When she asked Johnny to join her there, he could tell she'd been crying.

"You've got talent, son. I'm going to show you how to develop your own photos. Just don't tell your father."

Johnny hugged his mother and promised.

He picked his favorite possum photo and slipped it inside his bedside drawer. Every night before he went to sleep he stared at death, trying to understand what it meant.

10

I Miss Trees

Matthew Wallace

I miss the bird shit
Caked on my windshield.
I miss the red marks on my face
From branches and thorns.
I miss tripping on roots
And falling face first
Into muddy wet earth,
The earthworms would greet me on the way down.

Now my car is pristine,
Spotless, and I can see clearly.
I rake no leaves,
I fear no split trunk or fallen forestry,
But I miss the birds calls
And the earth worms,
How they loved me.
I miss the splintered life
Of trees.

11

Headless

Alena Graedon

I once dated a really handsome guy whose apartment was infested with bedbugs. I've heard it said that the most attractive people are those who don't know they're attractive, but I don't think that's true. People aware of their hotness keep on top of their dental hygiene. They get good haircuts, if they can afford to, and wear clothes in flattering colors and shapes. They know how to hold their faces, which expressions are sexy, how to catch the light. Vanity can be like makeup. It can make a person two degrees cuter than they would be otherwise.

When I met the handsome guy, Nick, at a Williamsburg bar, it was clear that he knew he was hot. His dark hair flopped over his forehead, and he wore a ragged blue shirt that favored his arms. His chunky black glasses made his Roman nose look even more delicate than it would have naked. They highlighted his high cheekbones and green eyes. It was his mouth, though, that was the giveaway. His smile was immaculate, like the smile on a joke-store skeleton. His teeth were white and straight. His lips were thick as profiteroles. When he wasn't smiling, he pouted them.

We'd been set up by a friend. Actually, I used to date the friend, Paul. Paul had planned the setup with a different friend he'd dated, and *she* used to date Nick. I have a theory about setups: we only arrange them for people we'd like to sleep with ourselves. When I shared my theory with Nick, which I did right away, as soon as we were seated outside with our drinks, I learned that his friend still texted him late at night. She wrote *I miss you* and *Want to come over?* Things like that. "That's funny," I said, "because, guess what? Me too, from Paul." We toasted to our friends still wanting to fuck us.

Nick was forthcoming about his bedbugs. One of his roommates had brought a couch in from off the street, he explained. Normally, words like bedbug and roommate didn't work on me as aphrodisiacs, but I'm not too proud to confess that attraction had rendered me brainless. I wanted to feel the profiterole lips. I also wanted, if I'm being honest, to prove to myself that I could date a man who looked like

Nick. I was pretty average-looking at best. I was also three years older than him, 36.

He assured me that the bedbugs were long gone, but he hadn't been willing to part with his extensive collection of books from the New York Review, which predated the infestation. To be safe, he stored them in large plastic bins beneath the lofted bed in his room. On our first date, he flashed me a photo of them, as if they were a baby or dog. I saw them with my own eyes just a week later, the first time I went to his place. "Wow, yeah," I said. "There they are." Their colorful jackets and spines— hunter green, navy blue, mustard, aubergine, maroon—looked solemn stacked in tight columns beneath the foggy plastic lids. I wondered if he ever read any of them.

When we'd walked into his apartment together, after getting a coffee, we'd waved awkwardly to a few of his roommates before making our way to his makeshift door, which was more like a board that sort of slid into place. It was hot in the lofted bed. It was summer, and his room didn't have AC. We pulled off our sticky tees and cutoff jeans, hunched over so we wouldn't hit our heads on the ceiling. His body was as I'd imagined it: lean, like an alpine skier's, without much hair. He had a tan line around his biceps from running outside each day in a shirt. We kissed and sucked each other's sweaty nipples for a while, and then he went down on me. I offered him a blowjob, but he declined politely.

As we lay there in the afterglow of my orgasm, I couldn't keep from thinking of the bins of books on the floor. I'd read somewhere that bedbugs could survive even sealed in plastic for six months. Was I being naïve to trust that they'd been eradicated? Was he? I kept imagining that I felt something crawling on me. I thought of friends who'd described their own infestations: the failed organic treatments, the noxious poisons, the dry-cleaning and laundry bills. All the things that had to be tossed, thousands of dollars and months lost. My clothes, in a puddled heap at my feet, worried me. When I got home that afternoon, I took them off in the kitchen, knotted them in a Glad, and took them immediately to the laundromat. I did this the next three times I went to Nick's. I also studied myself for bites, looking for small red dots in a line.

I lived alone on the top floor of a townhouse in Fort Greene. There were windows in every room. The kitchen was the size of a modest bodega, and the bathtub had claw feet. Just above me was a shared roof deck, though I was the only one who used it. My landlords, who lived downstairs, were so nice it was almost alarming. They hadn't raised my rent in the four years I'd lived there. They invited me to dinner about once a month, and, when I was away, watered my plants. Sometimes, they left fresh cookies on my doormat, or bottles of champagne labeled DRINK ME. It was the nicest place I'd ever lived, maybe the nicest place that existed, and during those first few weeks with Nick, I came up with increasingly implausible explanations for why he couldn't visit. I claimed that there was potting soil all over my kitchen floor. Then, that there was a strange chirping sound emanating from the walls. Then, that there was no water.

"You mean no hot water?" asked Nick. "No water at all."

He tried to convince me to stay at his place—"That's inhumane; sometimes our hot water is off, but never our water water"—and I realized that my ruse was dead.

"Actually, you know what?" I said. "I think it's back on. That's so strange. It's been off for days. Why don't you come here after all?"

He cooked chicken tikka masala, which we ate on the roof "al fresco," as Nick said. Nervous as it made me to let him stay—I eyed his backpack and clothes as if they were biohazard—we slept fairly peacefully. I woke up with no bites. He started staying over a few nights a week. We passed a month that way.

Then, on a night in early July when I was sleeping alone, I woke up to see a tiny black dot on the white expanse of my sheets. The dot was like a period. The sentence I'd been writing in my mind all this time had finally ended.

I fumbled in my office for tape. I didn't turn on the lights. If I kept the lights off, it was almost as if I was still asleep. I quickly entombed the dot, pressing the tape strip to cotton. I felt full of despair, like I was a despair water balloon, but I also felt tired and resigned. I dropped the taped bug on my kitchen table and then downed two sleeping pills. Back in my room, I pressed wax earplugs in my ears and donned an eye mask. I'll do anything, I thought, to lose consciousness. I wasn't an avoidant person generally, but I wanted to pretend, for one final night, that everything might be okay.

Before long, I managed to drop off, but a few hours later, I woke again. This time, something had bitten my ass. I felt a distinct sting in the skin. When I whipped the sheets back—sure enough, the same bugs. I taped all of them. It was 4 a.m. I thought, It's too bad I've just ruined my life. That might sound dramatic, but I really couldn't afford bedbugs then. I was in a lot of credit-card debt and unemployed. I'd been looking for a job for months. On top of that, I couldn't imagine facing my landlords. I'll be homeless, I thought. All for some cock.

I wrote Nick an email asking if he could walk me through what to do if I happened to have bedbugs. I was angry at myself for being so heedless. I couldn't believe I'd trusted him. It wasn't the first time that lust had detonated my reasoning faculties, but it was, so far, the most inconvenient.

I considered my options. Panicking at that hour was pointless, I told myself. What could I do? I wasn't going to wake my landlords with the vacuum. Laundromats and pest-control places were closed. So I took two more sleeping pills.

When I groggily woke at 10 a.m., I felt the panic waiting, pressing on the back of my skull like a hangover. I reached for my phone and saw five missed calls from Nick. He'd left an anxious message. Apparently, he'd biked to my apartment at 4:30 a.m., in the rain, and had rung my bell several times. I hadn't heard him through the layers of wax and benzodiazepine. When I hadn't answered, he'd biked home. He was now nervously waiting to hear from me.

Before I called him back, though, I made an unforeseen discovery. On my way to the bathroom to pee, I walked past my kitchen table and saw the stack of fossilized bugs. Bending down to study them, I noticed something odd: they didn't seem to have heads or legs. I then noticed something else: there was a cluster of these same headless bugs on the floor. I stooped down, pressed a finger to one, and examined it. It was then that I remembered the previous morning: I'd opened an industrial-sized bag of chia seeds. Because I'd never poured a large bag of chia seeds before—chia seeds aren't actually something I eat, but I'd thought, fleetingly, that I should—I'd spilled some. A chia seed is about the size of a freckle, oblong and dark, the color of ash. I'd promised myself, rushing out the door to a job interview, that I'd clean them up when I got home, but I forgot. And then, apparently, I'd stepped on them barefoot before getting into bed.

The relief was like warm honey in my blood. It was worth the anxiety. I wasn't exactly glad that this misunderstanding had happened, but afterward, I liked Nick even more. It was like I'd encountered him in a dream. Some of the goodwill contrails into reality. Whenever I have sex dreams, I lust over my dream partner for days, especially if it's a person I've never thought of that way before.

"The princess and the chia seed," I said when I finally called Nick back. He had no idea what I was talking about.

"Like the princess and the pea?" But he still didn't know, so I relayed the fable.

A prince long in search of a wife finds her at last when a strange girl, who claims to be a real princess, turns up in a storm on the castle steps. The queen proves the girl's identity by placing a pea in her bed beneath 20 mattresses and 20 eider-down beds. Because the girl is delicate enough to feel it—in fact, she gets marked black and blue—the queen knows she's telling the truth. "Nobody but a real princess could be as sensitive as that," she says.

I wish I could say that I learned a lesson from this, like the kind that fables are supposed to impart. I wish I'd never again falsely accused anyone or did something stupid for sex. But I didn't learn a lesson. In fact, things got worse for me before they got better.

12

Mother Wolf

Savannah Brooks

Once upon a time, there was a princess who wanted to be an artist.

The king and queen had had a slew of sons, and then, years later, a miraculous little girl. Because the princess had three older brothers, her parents weren't focused on her romantic prospects just yet, and so they encouraged her talent. Day after day, the princess sat by the treeline of the woods and sketched what she saw: warblers, porcupines, swallowtails, and—after she'd been sitting still and silent for hours—wolves. They were her favorite; their faces were the most expressive.

Happy years passed this way, but all good things come to an end—and in this case, it was a violent end. The princess was still relatively young when her kingdom was usurped, and there was the understanding that, when she came of age, she would be married off to the usurper's son.

When the family took her in, they also took her drawing pencils, her sketchpads, her time next to the woods. They gave her a portfolio of botanical illustrations to look at instead. They confined her to her room and told her all she needed to focus on was learning how to be a good wife. For the most part, she did just that, though occasionally a small sketch snuck out.

After a lifetime and no time at all, she was old enough to marry. She didn't understand what had changed, at first. She'd woken to a chilly, sticky patch on the back of her nightgown. When she panicked at the sight of so much blood, her chambermaid glowed and explained what this meant—the princess was ready to be a mother!—but that only made the princess feel chillier and stickier.

Over the years, the princess had grown accustomed to loneliness, but she hoped her wedding day would be different, and maybe even the days that followed. She hoped that, as the years passed, she and the usurper's son would develop a genuine fondness for each other. She hoped that he would treat her as a princess by her own right, not simply a producer of more princesses.

She should have known better.

Once her husband was getting something from her whenever he visited her bedchambers, though, the princess thought she might be able to ask something of him in return. Just a sketchpad, she explained, a couple of drawing pencils, maybe even some time outside of her room for artistic inspiration. A silly little hobby, but one that brought her great joy, she explained. He would make her such a happy wife.

But the only wife the usurper's son wanted was one he could keep in a cage—not to lock her in but to lock the world out.

"You have everything you need to be happy," he said, and he refused to bring her anything at all.

That was okay, the princess told herself. She'd lived without art supplies for this long; it wasn't ideal, but she could make do with what she had.

Her husband didn't like that she wasn't playing his game, though. In a fit, he stripped her room of anything she could conceivably create with, not just her quill nibs and ink pots, but loose paper, candle wax, charcoaled remnants from the fireplace. If she wanted those things, he told her, she would have to earn them.

She didn't want them that badly.

Her lonely life became even lonelier. Her husband found her so unappealing he only visited her once a month, during her most fertile time. He never spent the night, and she was glad for it.

Month after month, she awoke to blood on her sheets. Month after month, her husband scoffed.

"What are you good for?" he asked.

Cut off from people and art and warblers and porcupines, she honestly didn't know. She didn't feel much like a princess anymore, nor a girl, nor a wife. She didn't even feel like an artist, which was the only thing she had ever wanted.

If only she could draw again, she wouldn't feel so abstract.

And then she realized that she could, once a month.

She didn't need graphite or charcoal or even ink. She didn't need her husband to bring her anything at all. Her body would be its own fountain.

The first night of her next cycle, she drew a furtive wolf behind her bed, its coppery red eyes gleaming. The next night, another, this time with a bloody snout peeking out from the foot of her curtains. Then another, sitting vigil behind the door. One sniffing around her armoire. Another, and another, and another.

Seven nights; seven wolves. All untouchable, hidden away from him. Her room stank, fresh and metallic and deliciously wild, and she luxuriated in the baseness of her body.

By the time her husband came to her again, he wrinkled his nose.

"Wash up next time," he said, and the princess knew she would not. If he were going to take her anyway, he would have to take her as she was.

Seven wolves turned to fourteen turned to twenty-one. Three months had passed, and the townspeople were starting to wonder: Why wasn't she with child yet? Was something wrong with her?

The princess doubted she was so lucky. Eventually, she would bring a child into the world, a creature she couldn't hide away, that she couldn't protect.

"If only I could keep from getting pregnant," she lamented to her walls. "Not with him."

The next morning, she woke to a flat cluster of tiny white blossoms sitting on her windowsill. Which was odd, since her window was bolted shut and her door locked from the outside and she hadn't heard anyone come in.

A mystery was a very exciting change of pace, and as luck would have it, the usurper's family had accidentally given her just what she needed to solve this one. From the collection of botanical illustrations, she plucked just the page she needed: *Daucus carota*.

The princess had heard of wild carrot, but only in pinched whispers. When a girl found herself in a certain situation, people said, or if she had regrets about even the possibility of a certain situation. There was a way you could take care of things. There was a way you could stack your odds against this most natural of repercussions.

When the princess added seven more wolves to her walls, she rejoiced in the certainty of another generation—just not the one her husband was expecting. The princess would fill her own world with life; let him be responsible for what happened in his.

Her twenty-eight wolves multiplied into forty-two. They snooped around her fireplace, lolled against the molding, stretched up on her door frame. She had quit trying to hide them; her husband only saw her in the dark, anyway.

Each month, the night after her husband took his leave, the wild carrot appeared. Each month, she conjured seven more children.

After six more months had passed, though, her husband had exhausted his patience.

"If we don't conceive now, it will be the last time we try," he warned.

In the morning, she delighted in the wild carrot, cozy among her feral walls. She was more than happy to never try and conceive a child with him again.

But that wasn't what her husband meant.

The first night of her next cycle, as the princess drew her blood wolf, someone unlocked her bedroom door. When her husband walked in, his intent was clear—both in the cruelty on his face and the blade in his hand.

She froze. No one had ever taught her how to save herself. Her husband was strong and rich and powerful; she was simply his delicacy.

She closed her eyes, resigned to her fate.

That's why she didn't see the walls snarl to life around her. She heard them, though. The floor thundered against her feet as two hundred plate-sized paws launched into the room. She snapped her eyes open and tried to make sense of the pure chaos: wolves darting every which way, bowling each other over, bounding out her bedroom door. She put the scene into focus right as a handful flanked her husband.

Even if she could have looked away in time, she would never have been able to drown out his scream. It went on and on.

Why hadn't anyone come to check on them? she wondered. Her husband's cries rang through the corridors; surely someone had heard.

The princess waited as the wolves devoured their victory, but no one showed up. She waited as the wolves licked their bloody paws clean, but no one showed up. She waited as the wolves paced, restless, their haunches quivering with the ache to run, but no one showed up.

Finally, she stepped out of her cage.

As she passed room after room, she realized why no one had shown up: their bodies were scattered across the castle, their executioners still gorging. Snouts red and snapping, these wolves didn't feel any shame for what they had done. They didn't even understand the concept.

The princess wondered if she could ever be just like them: powerful and radiant and free. Once she passed both the king and queen's quarters, she realized that, yes, she could; everyone who would imprison her was dead.

She'd been a princess by both blood and marriage, but she was a queen by might. And over the years, with her wolves by her side, she became mighty indeed. Though her constant companions looked frightening, they were docile unless commanded otherwise—and they were hardly ever commanded otherwise. The queen was a very different kind of ruler than the usurper had been.

When Death began to shadow her, the queen called in her advisors and told them her plan: having no heirs of her own, she would choose the next queen—but at least half of her advisors would have to approve her appointment. The majority of her most trusted people would need to agree on who could best lead them.

This was a radical shift, they warned her. Such a big change might be difficult for the people.

She knew. But she also knew it wasn't as big of a change as a good kingdom being handed down—or handed over—to a bad ruler.

So, she was sure? her advisors wanted to know.

Yes, she was sure.

"Sometimes," she explained to her advisors, "the beasts we create in our imaginations are the most powerful beasts of all."

13

Caribbean Blue

Sara Shea

Sailing the West Indies
on a sea smooth as shark skin,
blue as a peacock's eye,
we drop anchor
in Oppenheimer Cay.

Iguana eyes gleam,
gold as plutonium,
from tangles of sea grape branches.
Lessons of Trinity, Hiroshima,
Nagasaki haunt memory.

A molasses sun drizzles into
ripening nutmeg drupes.
Palm fronds in the wind
are maracas and flamenco skirts.
Angelfish, lionfish, sea fans are
nature's calypso dancers.

At dusk, we dive off the bow
into a nexus of bioluminescence.
The father of the atomic bomb
escaped here, to this safety
of island paradise,
far removed from humankind.

I conjure mushroom clouds,
while we whisper
about mushroom tea
and full moon parties at Bomba's.

A man-o'-war drifts in trade winds.
Weapons lurk below.

The moon rises above
plumes of smokey evening clouds
that detonate and dissipate,
like octopus ink.

14

Reflections From the Eastern Continental Divide

Sara Shea

November 2024, post-Hurricane Helene

The full Frost moon spills fractured light
From a Sea of Tranquility tonight
here, over the Eastern Continental Divide
where water tumbled wild and wide.

Where Hickory Creek and Broad River surged
through raw ravines where waters merged
Down from Rattlesnake's rugged crest,
Raven Rock, Bald Knob attest—

Land broken by what it could not keep -
water that carried what's much too deep.
Boulders scattered like unfinished thoughts,
craters etched by the loss it wrought.

Logs jammed, banks ripped wide,
homes and highways tossed aside
Bridges broken, slopes stripped bare
to raw bedrock, mud, and mountain air.

A flood won't heal, but it unveils—
What bends, what breaks, and what prevails.
A landscape shaped by all it lost,
A soul defined by what it's crossed.

15
Swamp Lily

Sara Shea

I was eight, barely old enough to know
more than the shape of my own wonder -
skipping home from second grade
in galoshes, parka zipped to my chin.

I ducked beneath gnarled laurels,
crawled the narrow, secret path
past the swamp - black vernal pools
whispering between the school grounds
and the wide, quiet lawns
of our Connecticut street.

It was March, a time when trees stood bare,
when crusts of snow clung to shadowed gullies,
and the world felt half-dreamed and half-awake.

I lingered at the edge - took a hesitant step
toward dark water, where wonder
still lay submerged; a half-remembered song.

In summertime, magic had reigned here
when dragonflies danced like living jewels,
and pollywogs surged. I'd unearthed snails,
newts, traced raccoon tracks, glimpsed herons.

Now the swamp lay hushed.
I tested icy fringes. Slick black muck
crept past the cuff of my boot.
Then from the mire an unbidden shimmer:
a dark spire, purple as a bruise,
tender and obscene as a tongue.

Something luminous rising
against winter's dull palette.
A beast's horn? A hawk's hooked beak?
Silken slipper of a sleeping elf?
Its mystery was enough.

I pried that smooth, feral treasure
from the swamp's cold clutch,
gagging at its fetid breath-
garlic, earth, death, and birth -
and carried it home to my father,
who turned it in his hands, then smiled
at this secret only seasons could know-
"Ah, springtime… the skunk cabbage spathe."

16

The Psychopomp

Elizabeth Rae Bullmer

Is never still. Death's frequency,
forever flits from corpse to corpse.
They conduct their ceaseless symphony
of souls, swinging scythe or incendiary sword,
fantasizing fields of yellow wildflowers.

When they come for me, I will not plead
nor barter for time. I will not ask questions;
I know they cannot speak to the dead. Instead,
I will offer the battered bones of my abandoned body
for their collection, fistfuls of wood sorrel and goat-weed.

17

Do We Inherit the Way We Die?

Elizabeth Rae Bullmer

My family likes to die when the sun dances
high in its power—languid waltz of Equinox,
bright jitterbug or flashy foxtrot of Solstice,
dark tango of Samhain, when
the flimsy veil flirts between dimensions.

I finger the feathery fringe of my own mortality,
roll the lacy weave between my fingers
like the stiff shuffle of pages pinned with old
photographs—all that's left, once
clothes are donated and bones burned.

I've decided to leave at Midwinter,
gather the icy web of my darkest days to wrap
around my shoulders in shimmering strands;

walk straight into endless Spring peas
in pirouette, fluted hats atop jaunty jonquils
and the deep indigo blink—oceans of crocus.

18

Please Define the Word Legacy

Elizabeth Rae Bullmer

If the dead forget the living,
    even as they are remembered,
    are both only half who they once were?

What happens to memories eaten by mind?
    Lacy framework of a moth-nibbled shawl
    void of the storied hands that worked the weave.

If I am the keeper of my own history—
    if I choose to hold only what I need
    to love myself through this life, choose
    to see myself only as I aspire to be—

would it matter if I am remembered at all?

19

Ophelia: A Christmas Special

ZiXuan Angel Xin

> Trigger Warning - Rape, sexual assault

SYNOPSIS: When OPHELIA HWANG, an aspiring playwright, receives a mysterious phone call from her fiancé, HAMLET CHAMBERS, buried memories resurface.

CHARACTER:
COUNSEL - in her early twenties, woman and person of color.
ENSEMBLE - three to five women. All people of color.
HAMLET CHAMBERS (he/him) - in his late twenties, tall, caucasian man.
OPHELIA HWANG (she/they) - in her late twenties, short, Asian woman.

SETTING: In the waiting area of the airport. A week before Christmas Eve, post-COVID.

Playwright's Notes: All members of the Ensemble wear gray t-shirts. When Ensemble is called upon, the script invites all members of the Ensemble on stage. When Ensemble 1 is used, the script directs one member of the ensemble to take the stage.

Scene 1

Stage is dimly lit and empty. Counsel wanders into the scene from the front row of the audience, looking confused. He surveys the audience. Spotlight follows him.

COUNSEL.

(quietly, to herself) Goddamn– Really, this many people? Observing a proceeding on Christmas Eve?

The crowd is bustling: people shout, phones ring, aircraft fly in and out overhead. Volume of ambiance rises dramatically as we hear an aircraft land. COUNSEL stays seated, scrolling on her phone, undisturbed by the chaos. ENSEMBLE floods the stage– stopping to check their watch at times, and dragging their carry-ons as they frantically find their way to their respective gates. Various airport PSAs are broadcast. OPHELIA stands upstage, beneath a huge sign saying 'My Duty Free', holding a paperback book while carrying a half-zipped backpack and a tiny suitcase. A shrill ringing sound catches her attention. She picks up the phone.

COUNSEL.

(takes a long breath, loud and clear) Your honor, ladies and gentlemen of the jury, the prosecution would have you believe that Ophelia Hwang is guilty of a crime as horrific as violating Exodus 20:13. But today, we shall prove that my client is not guilty– *(towards the stool on the upstage left and down)*. Now let's set the scene.

OPHELIA.

Hey honey– what's up?– Ham?

(Ophelia clumsily scavenges through her backpack for a pen. She scans the stage, rushes over to secure a seat in the waiting area. Ophelia begins to annotate her book. Hamlet slowly walks into the scene from backstage. He holds his phone to his ear and sighs.)

HAMLET.

When should I pick you up from the airport?

OPHELIA.

Silly– I'm heading to my mom's place in Wisconsin first.

HAMLET.

(annoyed) But you promised to spend Christmas this year with my family– you know how much my mom *adores* you– and how much Christmas *means* to them.

OPHELIA.

(chuckling) Don't get yourself all worked up. Christmas is in a week! I'll be by your side before you even know it *(grimaces at a line building up in front of the boarding gate)*. Babe, can I call you back later?

HAMLET.

Hey – before you go, one last thing *(takes a deep breath)*.

OPHELIA.

(sarcastic) Ooo– mysterious! Is this my early Christmas present?

HAMLET.

I wouldn't exactly call this a gift *(sigh)*. Look, I just need a favor. This all happened when I was still in college— I was just a kid doing some self exploration, you know? *(chuckles)* Like the Age of Discovery—Christopher Columbus? Get it? I was out there claiming exotic territories.

(Hamlet laughs uncontrollably and slaps his own leg. Ophelia stands gaping. After realizing that she is uncomfortable, he finally stops.)

HAMLET.

What's wrong?

OPHELIA.

(horrified) There is nothing– and I mean it– *nothing* entertaining about rape culture and colonialism.

COUNSEL.

I second this.

HAMLET.

(mumbles to himself) There is not a single funny bone in you.

OPHELIA.

Hamlet Chambers? *(annoyed)* Wanna share your thoughts with the class?

HAMLET.

(clears his throat) After you broke up with me–

OPHELIA.

(interrupts) Because you ghosted me– but continue.

HAMLET.

So– after you broke up with me, I slept around. *(pause)* I *only* did that to get over you.

OPHELIA.

I really don't care about your past. History is everything that has happened. *(softly)* I only care about the future we are about to flesh out together.

HAMLET.

No, no– no. I need you to understand the context.

OPHELIA.

Context? You were a *pledge master.* I know who I'm getting myself into.

HAMLET.

Yeah– right *(grins)*. You girls all love that– but seriously– these sorority girls swarm around me like flies.

OPHELIA.

Now that's narcissism.

HAMLET.

No seriously. Women in this generation lack etiquette– forget the importance of self-preservation. Every single girl on that college campus walks out as a whore. It's damn right that college prepares women for brothels more than motherhood.

OPHELIA.

(frustrated, almost screaming) And that's because self-preservation is *impossible*. It is never a victim's burden to explain why they didn't consent. And it's the perpetrator's duty to–.

HAMLET.

(cuts her off) So you are saying that when a girl comes up to *me, flaunting* her cleavage– I shouldn't give her what she wants? Don't be ridiculous.

OPHELIA.

(audibly gasps) Flaunting?

HAMLET.

I could see her *cleavage. Exposed.* Her tits were *shaking* when she was walking towards me.

OPHELIA.

her– who *exactly* are you referring to?

HAMLET.

Well see, I was very naive– and I wasn't the best at reading signals. So this girl *(takes a deep breath)* accused *me* out of all people. *(waits for Ophelia to speak)* Doesn't this sound absolutely preposterous? *(louder)* For raping her. And now I have to go to goddamn trial because of this shit.

OPHELIA.

(talks to herself) No.

(Counsel runs offstage, seemingly shaken.)

HAMLET.

Right? We've been dating on and off for what– seven years? You knew me in high school. You know that I wouldn't possibly do that. It was consensual– and she's blaming it on the *alcohol*— But you see, I knew that she *wanted* it. She showed up at the frat in lingerie for God's sake.

COUNSEL.

(screaming from offstage) You– out of all people– knew that I *never* wanted it. I never *asked (snickering bitterly)* for it.

(Counsel enters slowly, seeming very collected, until they stand in the spotlight. Ophelia and Hamlet. freeze. Counsel drops to her knees.)

COUNSEL.

(calmly) I *begged* you. I *crawled* towards you. *Kneeled* before you. I told you to stop. I *screamed* for help– but you kept going– until you forced it down my throat. Until there was nothing left in me. Your honor, I was on my way to be a lawyer– to use my voice as a weapon to attack, and– of course– protect. But at that moment– I had no well of sound to draw from. *(breathing rapidly)* He took my voice away. Excuse me– your honor–

(Counsel stands up and returns to her seat. Ophelia and Hamlet unfreeze.)

HAMLET.

C'mon. We grew up together. You know that I wouldn't force myself on her. It was consensual– she probably doesn't even *remember* what happened– she blacked out already when it happened.

OPHELIA.

But she couldn't have consented if she was under the influence.

HAMLET.

(matter-of-factly) Everyone was drunk. Her boobs were *spilling* out of her top.

OPHELIA.

So you raped her *(long pause)*. Answer me. Ham? *(shaking)* Answer the fucking phone Hamlet.

OPHELIA squats down, her palms holding her temple.

COUNSEL.

Just like that– with the snap of a finger– Ophelia becomes *me*. Her body aches under foreign skin, rubbing against alien cement. Somehow– the beauty belonging to two textures of skin sharing the same rhythm and temperature became a crime. She tries to erase the image of her fiancé shamelessly *drilling* his nail into a newly plastered wall. She carried his crime– like a sin on her back.

HAMLET.

You can't be fucking serious right now– you're taking her side over mine? I am your fiancé– get a grip.

OPHELIA.

(crying and shaking) Does mom know about this?

HAMLET.

(quietly) Yes

OPHELIA.

Mom. *Your Mom.* Knows?

(Ophelia slowly pulls out a transparent yellow bottle of pills from her pocket. She stares intensely at the bottle, pacing around, and she puts the bottle back in her pocket.)

HAMLET.

And why is that so hard to believe?

COUNSEL.

In *Hamlet*, Ophelia found it hard to believe that Hamlet, the love of her life, murdered her own father, Polonius.

(Ophelia paces around, and leans against an aisle selling flight necessities. She curls up her knees and takes a deep breath.)

COUNSEL.

Now, Ophelia found it hard to believe that Hamlet, the love of her life, is a rapist. Ophelia refused to believe that Gertrude, her mother in law, out of all people, would stand by Hamlet's actions. After all, she was a woman before she became a mother.

HAMLET.

She is my mother. Of course she chose to protect her son over some *(scratches his head)* slut.

OPHELIA.

(chokes) slut?

HAMLET.

Just quit it. Quit the morally superior facade that you always have on. Gosh if this scene happened in the Bible, you would be the Virgin Mary for Jesus' sake. But all of this– all of this– it's ridiculous to me how you can care more about a *stranger* than your own fiancé.

OPHELIA.

No, no, no– this isn't about who I'm closer to – it's about having enough critical thinking skills to discern the victim from the perpetrator.

COUNSEL.

Clock him.

HAMLET.

(shouting) I just need an alibi. Look, if you said that we were getting dinner together that evening– we can erase– forget everything that happened. We can start our life in a clean state. Think about the child in your belly.

COUNSEL.

But see– that's exactly what perpetrators always forget. Trauma can never be erased. I died with the shame, guilt, and pain cemented in his crime. For years, I kept on reliving that singular, terrible hour.

OPHELIA.

I can't do this. *(sobbing)* I'm sorry. Perhaps I don't know her– but I am a woman. I feel her plight.

HAMLET.

She's dead already for God's sake. She killed herself– couldn't accept the consequences of her *own* actions.

OPHELIA.

(physically shaking) No.

HAMLET.

(softly) Ophelia. *(frustrated)* Stop fucking crying. You are a grown woman. Look at me.

(Ophelia stands up and walks towards Hamlet. Hamlet walks towards Ophelia. A glass screen separates them.)

HAMLET.

That's right. We will be raising a family together. You have always wanted this– a complete and functional family.

OPHELIA.

(wavering) Yes–

HAMLET.

And when was the last time you saw your father? Or should I say– visited his grave?

OPHELIA.

Hamlet. Please. Stop this.

HAMLET.

I won't stop until you say yes.

OPHELIA.

But making up an alibi– lying under oath– *(stutters)* it's perjury. *(hesitates)* You know that if I get caught– who knows, my Christmas present might be a jail sentence, right? My future would practically be gone. *(tries to wipe away her tear but it keeps on flooding)*

HAMLET.

(imitates Ophelia's more elevated pitch) what if *I* get caught– Goddamn it. What if *I* get caught. I will be sentenced for– I don't even know how long. *(sighs)* Sometimes I really think that you spend so much time with Shakespeare, you forget that you exist in the *real* world. You're not Ophelia– in what book is it– *Macbeth*?

OPHELIA.

You can't say his name– it's an ill omen *(sighs)*. But no it's not Macbeth– we *literally* watched this production together at the Globe– remember? You proposed to me later that evening!

HAMLET.

Right– Hamlet. The *to be or not to be* bullshit.

OPHELIA.

Language!

HAMLET.

But seriously– you want me to end up like him? Live out his tragedy for comical purposes?

OPHELIA.

(frustrated) It's just a name. Names don't mean anything.

COUNSEL.

And here is where I interject. Names hold power. My client's name tethered her story to Ophelia's fate. In *Hamlet*, Ophelia didn't just go mad like– *poof and voila*– rather, her grief and inability to enact change fucked her over. Ophelia didn't have the guts to avenge a wrong, when someone whom she loved was a perpetrator. She chose death. It was as simple as that. *(sits back down on the stool)*

HAMLET.

What I meant to say is that this is our life– not some high school theatre production. You aren't some wacky main character that gets to do whatever she wants. You don't exist in a vacuum. You live in the real world– where you have to think about– you know– things, people– other than yourself. The child that you are carrying in your stomach never did anything wrong.

OPHELIA.

You couldn't control your fucking dick– and that *killed* her. You fucked her life over– so it isn't rocket science that you– out of all people– *should* take responsibility. Our baby is innocent– but you aren't!

HAMLET.

But I *can't* go to jail. I am the one with a future in this family, leading the family that assigned you value. I am the one that could make it into the big leagues– make a fucking difference. *(shuffles his hands for warmth)* Let's face it, no one gives a fuck about your thesis– big blank paragraphs of pessimism mocking the pastry-dorkies [patriarchy]. *(takes a hit from his vape)* Why would *anyone*– and I mean anyone with the right mind– waste their time digesting your bullshit.

OPHELIA.

It's the patriarchy.

HAMLET.

Doesn't matter. I am your man. I will do anything in my power to protect this family. Our family.

(Ophelia hangs up and furls her body into a ball. The light shining on Hamlet dies. He exits the stage.)

Scene 2

Stage dims. Spotlight follows Ensemble as they enter from the audience. Ensemble takes turns fiddling with the suitcase and travels across the stage dragging the luggage, as if Ophelia's carry-on is a member of their troop.

OPHELIA.

Jesus Christ. *(stares at the dancing Ensemble in horror).* It's moving. My suitcase– it's moving on its own. It has a life of its own!

ENSEMBLE1.

Accomplice!

(Ophelia runs across the stage, barefoot, following behind the rest of the Ensemble, lifting the luggage in their arms as they encircle Ophelia. Spotlight focuses on Ophelia.)

OPHELIA.

What do you want from me? *(takes a step back, facing the audience)*

(Ensemble takes a step towards Ophelia.)

OPHELIA.

(shaking) Tell me– I'll do as you say.

ENSEMBLE2.

Make a *good* choice– make the *right* choice.

(Ensemble takes another step, coming closer toward Ophelia.)

OPHELIA.

Even Hamlet's father gave him a tangible to-do list– am I right? That *if thou didst ever thy dear father love– revenge his foul and most unnatural murder!* There's nothing about the diction *right* that's tangible? You see, to be *good* and *right* would be completely different for a utilitarian and a deontologist. Would the Fates even reach a unanimous decision? *(talks to the audience)* I have no fate, no scheme to revenge– nothing but madness in my grasp! Please, help me, God. Tell me what to do.

ENSEMBLE3.

Do as Hamlet says.

OPHELIA.

But I can't possibly do that. In doing so I will be making a statement, publically announcing my personal stance– that it is morally permissible to rape. I will be standing against a crime which I have been a victim of. *I will not forgive myself.*

(Stage dims. Spotlight follows Counsel as they enter from the audience. Ophelia and Ensemble freeze.)

COUNSEL.

And that's when it dawned on her. This *something* that didn't feel right– this out-of-body experience wasn't a package deal that came with Ophelia's super-human empathy system. It was a nightmare that she *lived* through– buried so deeply inside of her that she forcibly *forgot*– scratched out from her memory. Now that it– the slit of nightmare– finally fled the safe– Ophelia was back in high school.

(Ophelia unfreezes, staring into a mirror. She takes off her jacket and steps out of her sweatpants, revealing a girl in her undergarments. She shrieks and covers her own ears.)

COUNSEL.

Hamlet and Ophelia had been dating for a few months already when he asked her to guide him through her body. He told her that he loved her. He demanded her to love him back.

(Ophelia smashes the mirror continuously until the mirror breaks into a thousand different pieces. More mirrors enter the stage, reflecting Ophelia's figure from multiple directions.)

COUNSEL.

And when she didn't have enough love to lend him a space inside of her, he forced his body in.

(Spotlight focuses on Ophelia as she collapses to the floor.)

COUNSEL.

He confused physical intimacy with war– for him and a sea of men on the same cruise: love is a commodity that any man can thrust upon any woman *(long pause)*. See– in every play, novel, film alike– the villain has a backstory that makes them morally sympathizable. We try to justify their crimes by humanizing them. But the thing is, rape is never morally ambiguous– morally comprehensible. A backstory is never an excuse to perpetrate harm.

(Hamlet enters. Spotlight focuses on him, waving victoriously to the audience like a general. Counsel drags him off the stage.)

COUNSEL.

Ophelia never forgave him. She simply lied to herself so persistently that nothing had ever happened.

OPHELIA.

Stop it. Stop it. This isn't real. I am in a dream– a nightmare. I just need to wake up.

(Ophelia frantically bangs her head against her suitcase.)

COUNSEL.

And the saddest thing of all– you honor– is that Ophelia wasn't in a dream. She isn't the main character of a novel– or a lead in a play.

Hamlet said this before me: Ophelia Hwang subsists in the real world. She sits in a crowd, watching play after play unfold.

OPHELIA.

So you're telling me that Hamlet's right? *(stutter)*– that I really am stuck in the past? But– but– where am I? Am I trapped in Shakespeare's play or the thunderous applause after my final high school theatre production– or the first time Hamlet *touched* me? How can I get out?

(Counsel stoops next to Ophelia and caresses her.)

COUNSEL.

Ophelia isn't a Shakespearean tragedy because she is alive. She is imprisoned– stuck– trapped– inside us. Whatever you want to call this. Ophelia is a tragedy without Shakepearean art– too raw and searing to be written in verses.

(Counsel exists. Ophelia sits on the seat in the waiting area of the airport she first sat in. Stage dims, the spotlight focuses on Ophelia.)

OPHELIA.

(raises a bottle of sleeping pills from her pocket.) To be or not to be? To free myself through death or stay in captivity? You see, when I think "death," I think *(pause)* the T.S. Elliot's metaphorical death of poetry, the fall of modernism – or *(stumbling on her words)* Paul De Man's proposition that metaphors have lost their footing in today's society. Death is grand, impersonal. *(louder)* And so fucking arbitrary. *And* in every single play that I have analyzed, death has always been a metaphor. Antigone's suicide, for one, is a metaphor for the ease it is, and perhaps the ease that always will be, for a man to silence a woman– yet when we gift suicide the title of martyrdom, human fragility and futility suddenly becomes holy? Now what would

my "death" serve as a metaphor for? *(chuckles softly)* A woman's final Christmas present to the patriarchy it subsists in? *(downs the entire bottle of pills and falls)*

Stage goes dark.

The End

20

Visual Art

Robin Young

Thanks a lot Ozempic, Collage, 9x8 inches, 2024

The Accordion, Collage , 8 x 10 inches, 2024

I Think I Can Make A Change, Collage, 8 x 8 inches, 2024

Mosaic of Shattered Dreams, Collage, 8 x 8 inches, 2024

The Midnight Sun, Collage, 8 x 10 inches, 2024

21

Cosmic

E. A. McCarthey

Black car seat leather stings my skin with the delicious heat of my seventeenth summer, a
>   freeingly oppressive heat like dinner rolls in an oven, baking alive and loving it.
>   If this car is Mars, I am a Martian.
My own home will never be home while this blazing comet best friend and her passenger seat
>   exist.

Junk food wrappers reign over their crooked kingdom from their cupholder throne, over chip bag
>   constituents and citizens of miscellany, 7-11 shelves emptied into her floorboards.
Fall Out Boy hums on the radio, a fragment of a distant cumulonimbus version of me.
We sing every word like a hymn in the finite endlessness of Saturday freedom, going nowhere
>   fast.

Plagued by some elusive rulebook, the Sphinx's riddle in glitter gel pen, by a hunger to grow and
>   the agony of growing up,
cured by her shooting star antidote. How is it
that some people know how to be human
better than others?

>   Personhood has always evaded me; Martianity beckons.
In this red steel, red-hazed Martian oasis, I am not the straight-A daughter graying by fifteen, not
>   the countdown to the cap and gown;
>   I am sleepover laughter at noon, a 5'7 renaissance, a raindrop monsoon of self after a
>   seventeen-year drought.

I have never known how to be a self, but in this steel haven, I don't need to be.
>   I only need the tinfoil hat attitude, tinfoil blanket, baked potato heat of this
>   bright red Mars rover
>   and the black leather convenience store kingdom
>   sprawled at my feet,
the sting of freedom on my skin and savory scent of my best bad decisions in the air,
the purring and rumbling of this cosmic carnelian car
under the sound of Saturday.

22

Bear Cave

E. A. McCarthey

My little sister's bedroom
has been vacant for six weeks
when I creep in on socked tiptoes
so my monsters under her bed
don't hear.

Weeds have burst through floorboards;
poppies grow in a ring around
where they found the empty pill bottle.
I want to drain my body of water,
replace it with lemonade
just so the pain will change.

Ivy creeps through the ancient window
my little Ophelia left open,
summer sun breaking
through January clouds;
but I'm still learning to swim
in the water over the bridge.

She's coming home tomorrow.

I take her crusty once-purple Care Bear
and prop her up against pillows
to keep watch.

Last month I swallowed poppy seeds,
squeezed them through my pores;
now they grow out through my skin,
eyes, ears, mouth, until
I can't breathe
and I'm leaking lemon tears.

I'm coming home tomorrow.

I lie in the shadow of her bed,
spread-eagle, dull star,
making Nothing angels
where we used to play with Barbies.

Teddy arms dig roots into me,
rake me across splintered floors,
tilling my flowerbed skin—
drag me under the bed, into their cave,
bury me under the floorboards
to hibernate.

She's coming home tomorrow.

23

Carnelian

E. A. McCarthey

It was raining when she crashed the car.
The hand-me-down planet from her mother had driven us across
every childhood galaxy and teenage travesty
until that drenched Tuesday mundicide,
when shards of our world fled the scene down I-35
with the wind as their accomplice.

She got a new car, a temporary heaven of grease and salt and fried
ambrosia,
sculpted of novelty and nostalgia.
We planted saplings that would grow into flags,
printed our feet in the
red soil that smelled like home
and squelched as our boots sank in.

That summer we spent Socratic circle sunsets crunching and
crashing and creating,
socked feet on the dashboard, headlights like glow worms,
crumbs in the seats clinging to our thighs like sand between toes,
sharing twin soliloquies like Phobos and Deimos locked in eternal
orbit—

An eternity destined to end.
When she blossomed and I realized I never would,
I learned this new car was Mercury,
too close to the sun;
that heaven was an empire
and empires fall.

Now I am the backseater, the pity invite,
the every-other-monther, the obligation, the memory,
always the childhood friend,
never a bridesmaid.

I am left behind, the last codependent crybaby of the endangered Martians,
tethered to echoes of Mars rover midnights
and Wal-Mart parking lots at 1am,
stuck counting constellations for eternity
in the ghost of this cosmic carnelian car,
clinging to memories like crumbs to thighs.

24

Self

John Pring

bacteria / rushes in / to multiply / chant / the name / of what / this is / the cost / of healing / flecked petals / of skin / but / no heaven / in the cut / unforge myself / wound / mouth / promises nothing / but / the morning

25

Anaphora as a Dying Son

John Pring

a country –

    my father's

        hands, rivers

            run to exhaustion

                across his palms

a map –

    my father's

        hands, roads

            carved with wheat

                blades inside the skin

a home –

    my father's

        hands, opening

            to welcome the

                unbearable softness

of a son

26

Coffee Date

Colton Johnson

CHARACTERS:

MARV- A 5'10 semi-built guy, looks beat up from the night before, presumably drunk, 5 o'clock shadow.

JAKE- A tall dorky guy, dressing semi-casual, excitement in everything to his posture

WAITRESS - A young female

ROBERT - An older male, manager of the coffee shop

SETTING: Coffee Shop

AT RISE: Marv walks in through the front door and sees his friend Jake sitting at a booth by himself. Jake is waving frantically at him to get his attention.

JAKE

Marv! Marv! You will not believe this shit, I swear

MARV

(Sits down across the table from Jake; he looks exhausted already)

What bro? You woke me up for this.

JAKE

Jesus, Marv, you look really awful, man. Everything alright?

MARV

Yeah eve-

(Marv cuts himself off and looks at Jake.)

(Cut to Jake, who is calling out the waitress loudly, not in a rude way, but in an enthusiastic way where everyone is staring at him.)

(The waitress finally gives him her attention and lets out a sigh.)

WAITRESS

What can I get you?

JAKE

(Looks at Marv) What do you want?

(Marv is still surprised. He looks at the waitress in fear as she angrily gazes into his eyes.)

MARV

Uhhhmmmm

(Marv looks slightly shaken.)

JAKE

Never mind him. Can we get two rum and Cokes?

WAITRESS

(Taken aback by the question)

Sir, it is *(looks down at watch)* 2:37 P.M. And we are at a coffee shop.

JAKE

(surprised) Do you know who we are?

(Waitress and Marv look super confused now, Waitress because she thinks she is supposed to recognize these guys, and Marv, because she isn't supposed to recognize them.)

WAITRESS

(Sarcastically) Well, who are you two fine gentlemen?

MARV

Just drop it, Jake. So sorry, can we get two coff-

JAKE

(Slams hands onto the table)

WE ARE THE CUTTING EDGE OF TECHNOLOGY!

(The whole place goes quiet for a brief second, with everyone looking over at these three in a standoff.)

WAITRESS

I'm getting my manager.

JAKE

(grimacing) Go right the fuck ahead.

The waitress walks away in a rush to get away from Jake and Marv. Jake has a huge smile on his face. Marv looks considerably pissed off about everything.

MARV

What is your fucking problem, dude?

JAKE

I had to get her away so I could tell you my idea. I'm telling you, dawg, it's top-secret shit.

MARV

Well, go ahead and tell me before we get kicked out.

(At that moment, the Waitress comes back with her Manager; the Manager looks angry at first, but his expression quickly changes.)

MANAGER

Holy shit! I am so fucking sorry, guys. Jesus Christ. I'm Robert, if you need anything.

WAITRESS

Wait? Who are these guys?

(Robert turns around, looks panicked.)

ROBERT

Get...

(calms down, takes a nice pause for himself) Get the fuck out...

WAITRESS

(crying) What...

ROBERT

Get...

(Waitress starts running out crying, grabbing her tips on the way out.)

ROBERT

I'll get you guys two loaded plates just one sec...

(Running into the kitchen)

GET ON IT RIGHT FUCKING NOW!

(Marv looks at Jake now with his eyes wide, astonished by what he's seen.)

JAKE

What is going on dude? Please just tell me why these people know us so I can go home.

JAKE

Ok so did you watch Shark Tank last night?

MARV

(Looking at him, scared now.) You didn't?!?

JAKE

Yup, and I told them it was our idea!

(Jake is holding his phone out to show Marv the clip from last night's episode.)

Int - Shark tank studio - night

JAKE

Alright sharks, today I bring you the whispering alarm clock.

(The Shark Tank cast is sitting there quietly, trying to analyze this weird product. Jake is of course, oblivious to this look of complete denial.)

JAKE

Ok, so me and my friend Marvin...

(pulls out photo of Marv and shows it to the camera)

Came up with this amazing idea and, well... only way to truly see it is to try it yourself.

(The alarm goes off that very second, with soothing Sade esc. Instrumentals and Jake's voice over on it.)

ALARM

Wake up beautiful. I miss you

(Jake looks at them for a quick second before the next audio line comes out.)

ALARM

Come on give me a hug, I want you up with-

Int. COFFEE SHOP - DAY

(Marv pauses the video right there. He's clearly angry and tired.)

MARV

I'm getting out of here.

JAKE

Wait but-

MARV

No... no I'm done

(Marv leaves Jake. Jake looks kind of sad now. Jake is alone at the table, pondering what his next move is, when Robert comes over and brings the two aforementioned plates.)

JAKE

(sadly) Thank you.

ROBERT

Don't be a sad kid. I see this happen all the time with revolutionaries like yourself.

(Jake pauses for a second before shedding a single tear and looking up at the man.)

JAKE

Thank you

(Robert nods his head and walks away; Jake pulls his phone out alone and skips ahead to the end of the video. All we can see is his face looking at his phone somberly.)

KEVIN (O.S.)

Looks like we have a deal, Jake. 4 million for 10 percent of the company.

JAKE (O.S.)

Me and Marv will not let you down sir.

The End

27
Bedtime

Michael J. Galko

I ate three
strawberries

by moonlight.
The first

was too ripe.
Also the second.

By the time
I finished the third

I had forgotten
what vexed me.

28

The Crazy Card is an Eleven of Hearts

Michael J. Galko

It doesn't look crazy at first. Just a little off.
It looks like a card with too many hearts. Blue ones.

On its back is a jack, not of hearts–
maybe of spades or clubs. The jack
is putting its lance tight to the neck of the joker.

The joker has fear in his eyes. The bells
on his jester's cap are ringing, a neck vein
is bulging as he leans away from the blade.
Interestingly, his stomach is a yellow diamond.

Look, I understand you are facing something hard.
And that heart can be read "hurt" with a certain accent
or lisp. Everyone has this card in their deck somewhere,
I know. But if you're going to actually *play* the crazy card, then please
deal me out. I've been that joker before. I've heard the bells. Next is
    blood on the floor.

29

The One Hundred and First Tale

Michael J. Galko

After Boccaccio's Decameron

I.
They finished the tales
as the sun stretched
orange-purple over the
gardens. The seven women
and three men rose and bloomed
out over the plague-ridden fields,
their erratic footfalls forming the
heartbeat of a new world.

II.
They cut each other garlands and
corsets of the greenest leaves and
yellowest flowers, pinning them
    with light fingers
on each other's breasts, singing
no dirges in their isolation.
   Converging on a quiet glade
they spread themselves out to dream
of their ten days together and those
who have wrought generously
    in matters of love.

III.
    Two did not dream,
tired of conjecture and example,
fearful of the impending return.
They rose up with locked hands
and passed the statues with the

cold but incensorious eyes like
those of the abandoned pestilent
dead, the mill with its familiar
hard floor bathed in soft dust
that clung to sweat like sweat
to the body, and the stream
babbling incoherently of
      previous illicit fordings.

IV.
They settled on a small enmossed
smokehouse, relic of a plentiful
time, still hung with pheasants,
fish, deer, and even a boar, all
of them brown and pungent,
heavy with the odor of the
moment before rot sets in.
The door they left cracked
for the dusky light as they
dropped their white robes
and sunk to the mossy floor,
entwining their pale legs
so it looked from outside
(where God might be watching)
like four large maggots crawling
luminescent among the decaying
meat, taking their pleasure the one
of the other, telling the tale that
            was omitted.

30

Real American Lover

Jacie Eubanks

Baby, you're cerebral; you're my Cape Cod Queen.
I see the red and the white gleaming
In your wide-toothed smile.
The bombs flew all night,
But I grew deaf from their wake.
The chemtrails just look like clouds from here, dear,
Smoke and ash never did any harm.
Kiss my bloodied knuckles,
Take the homegrown lead from my blood with your touch.
They're tattooed across the skin, the well-born prophecy—
The American Dream.
Like my forefathers before me,
I believed that there's no love like American love.

The seas are drying and the birds are crying,
But I've got the keys to my Cadillac 69'
And we'll be out all night drivin.'
The top is off, and the stars are shinnin'—
But don't you fret, girl,
Cause I've got the gun palm up standin.'
Won't you keep it safe for me, honey?
Hold it in your pretty little hand,
Because if I see 'em, I'll start shooting like a man.
I wouldn't even need to look,
The terror in your face is all that I believe.
I'll save you—
sunglass tint, eye in the rearview mirror—
you wouldn't even need to breathe—
Cause there's no love like American love.

Your daddy hates me real bad, darlin.'
He says I've got soft knees and rough palms
And a dirty look,

And God doesn't like none of that.
Says he can already smell the fires burnin.'
Well girl, our time is up—
I told y'a, I'm no man for you.
I'm all just dead ends and lame words.
I ate you up, I've had my fill,
And I don't care how it is.
You'll go back to your old man cryin,'
But by then it'll be too late for you,
And God doesn't want none of that.
There's no room for sinners,
and he can already smell the fires burning—
Cause there's no love like American love.

I'm all washed up like an earthbound whale,
White-bellied up and bloated.
Nothin' but pocket change
And loose-end pills from a kid no better off than me.
We'd smoke a few and hitch a ride,
Tripping through the seven seas.
I'd never felt better than that—
like a child on Christmas Eve—
I can't sleep; I can't wake.
Like a girl on her wedding day,
Eyes wide and shakin' hands.
I'll wake up in a week,
Wrapped in dirty rags and in the dark.
I'll never know where I am,
Cause there is no place for me.
I'm not the man I was,
Cause there's no love like American love.

One day I'll be so old and can't see straight.
I'll think I know cause I've made it to the end,
but I haven't got a clue.
My life is over, I've settled down,
but I'll still be screaming all day long
with nothing else to do.
The kids on TV and down the street,
They don't know none.
They didn't have it dirty like me;
They're all fighting for the wrong side.
They don't know that the old man never did wrong,
So they're throwin' hands and throwin' rocks.
Thinkin' that they're winnin,'
but they've got it all wrong—
Cause there's no love like American love.

I'll die penniless and alone,
My forgotten fresh made a blowfly express.
I'll sit for eternity in an unmarked grave,
Dead grass with kids kicking dirt in each other's eyes.
But this was my home, my firstborn, my wife, and my time.
I was a real piece of shit,
But I died and lived an American man.
I killed, I bled, and I fought—
or at least so I thought—
And at the end of the day,
I know that there's no love like American love.

31

The Hermaphroditic Seed

Jacie Eubanks

Oh, how they adored gloriant Aphrodite!
My dear mother, pickled sweet and fresh, as she was,
Once ago, dragged dripping from her sea-bed,
Born from her own anguished beauty.

And then came I, brought raw from the earth
And of the meaner sex—
She scooped me into her arms,
Her handsome, cherry-picked,
Half-man, half-woman child,
And cooed into my ample ear:

*"A mistake of life,
A mistake of love,
Are you, aren't you,
My dearest child?*

*From hence the river banks of
Greater Caria, she laid lusting
In her pool of greed
wishing to be forever united, entangled—
Praying to the gods
That there must be
a curse laid upon thee."*

And thus, I looked into the eyes
Of my dear and beautiful mother,
Her lashes glimmered, crystallized
in the sea-salt of all the tears she once cried.

And in her, I saw my reflection
And I wished my flesh was more of her own,
Dripping In all her poignant beauty
And less of him, tortured in a prison
Of a body that was never mine.

32

Inspector #1

John Delaney

Determined to get to the bottom of things,
the cat tests gravity by knocking off
a spoon from the table, watching it bounce
on the floor, then jumping down to paw it.
Once it passes inspection, he moves on.
But so much begs for attention, he can't
restore the order he is tasked to probe.

One of my new shirts had in its pocket
a little slip of printed paper,
saying it had been inspected by #1.
Watching the cat reminds me of that,
how one is reassured by a little proof,
repeating a simple test, giving a poke—
deciding what requires disemboweling.

Still, when you get down to the nitty-gritty,
admit cardboard is just cardboard, Kitty.

33

Adopting a Cat: Checklist

John Delaney

Taunts the long shadows with maudlin meows. √
Explores every nook and cranny. Canny. √
Finds hiding places in storage spaces. √
Resumes eating habits, with treating perks. √
Bears the litter box as daily detox. √
Toys with the joys of empty paper bags. √
Purrs pat approval of each petting pal. √
Sleeps to daydream and/or daydreams to sleep. √
Claws scratching post to exorcise his ghost. √
Curls a catnap around your tempting lap. √
Kneads on your chest his leavening dough. √
Gifts freely his love, offered a home of. √

Bless that kindness has found you and bound you.
Now tender your heart till death do you part. √√

34

What We Lose

Rowan Waller

when I was smaller
I could speak to animals
trace the origins of dragons
through glittery scale residue
on midtown windowsills
bisect the secrets of the universe
in intimate penned conversations with
neighborhood faye who collected
my wisdom and milk teeth
opened the chimney flue to welcome
the spirits of late December eves
deciphered codes from the
flashing of lights across night skies and in
the dotting of holes in mothworn coats

these days I have so little to offer
but apologies

35

Secrets Our Bodies Keep

Colleen S. Harris

My post-cancer hair grows back
Black and curly where a curtain
of mahogany hung.
You are not the first man
to enter my body, but
the cry I offer each time
we make love is one only
you have heard. I do not
know which stretch marks
belong to my daughters, or
to my son. There are scars
from wars I don't remember
fighting against pine trees,
crabs and kitchen appliances.
I reach out to touch a freckle
you do not know lives
on the curve of your ear,
and wonder if there is time
enough to discover all
the secrets our bodies keep.

36
Visual Art

Cynthia Yatchman

Mullet, alcohol inks and acrylic paint, 12"X 14", 2024

Torch, alcohol inks and acrylic paint, 14 "X 12", 2024

Cottage, alcohol inks and acrylic paint, 12" X 12", 2024

Fossils 2, alcohol inks and acrylic paint, 12" X 12", 2024

Burt, alcohol inks and acrylic paint, 12" X 12", 2024

37

Desolation

Lindsay Thurman

I refilled my glass with the cheap boxed wine in the fridge. I had grown accustomed to the taste since it was the only alcohol I could keep in the house that wouldn't disappear by the next morning. As I headed back to the living room, I tripped over the cat and licked the spilled wine off my forearm. The couch welcomed me back and I sank into the soft cushions as the cat settled in next to me. Her purring soothed the deep ache of my isolation, and I stroked her fur as I swallowed the cold and overly sweet wine that would soften the sharp edges of my reality.

He went out with his new friends who worked on base with him. The one time I'd met them, their disdain mirrored the complaints my husband regularly spewed about my appearance, personality, and intelligence. When he'd gotten dressed in jeans and a new shirt that looked like nothing more than a pathetic attempt to mimic the loud and gaudy style of his new coterie, I found one of the new movies I'd wanted to see that he preferred to miss. He opened the door and stepped outside but paused and turned back to say goodbye. I smiled and stood to offer a kiss, but he ignored my eager display of affection. Feeling foolish, I walked to the bathroom and splashed cold water on my face. Tears had pooled in the corners of my eyes as I gazed at my reflection. The heat of the West Texas summer made my hair frizz. I didn't bother with much makeup these days since any attempts at beautification often conjured cruel jabs. My baggy clothes hung heavy over my body, whose flaws were regularly pointed out. My appearance used to make him swell with pride, but now I was an embarrassment to my husband.

I closed my eyes and took another sip of wine. So much of my time was spent alone. The social aspects of life that I craved had become foreign and mildly terrifying. He always said that any job I could get wouldn't be worth the cost of getting a second car and going back to school would be too expensive, so I found ways to occupy my time. On Mondays, I cleaned the walls and windows, on Tuesdays I dusted, on Wednesdays I vacuumed, on Thursdays I cleaned the bathrooms, and on Fridays I did laundry. I read, painted, and watched the same syndicated shows in an endless loop. Each activity helped me find moments of sanity in the madness of infinite time.

I sighed as I ran through my agenda for my endless days of leisure. He regularly pointed out how I was completely reliant on him, and the weight of my failure was suffocating. I got more wine and moved outside to breathe the fresh night air. My mind drifted and as the alcohol numbed my defenses, I was reminded of the betrayal that had been lurking in the background for years. I'd been registering the new PlayStation console I got him for his birthday, and when I logged into his email to confirm the address, I noticed he had several messages from dating websites. My mouth turned sour as I scrolled through his inbox and read about the hundreds of women wanting to message him. He always used the same credentials, so I logged into each site and read the cringe-inducing bio he'd written for his profiles. He bragged about being able to show a woman a good time, especially in the bedroom. I thought it was brazen of him to proclaim he was a master of sensuality. I'd always made sure that he knew that I enjoyed our intimate moments, but I generally had to do most of the work. And even though I never brought it up because I loved him and didn't want to make him feel uncomfortable, I never understood why he always kept his underwear on.

Thankfully, he hadn't paid any of the fees that would allow him to communicate with anyone, but the raw deception sent a chill through my spine. I returned to his email and scanned through the endless ads until something else caught my eye. He'd been sending messages to one of my former bridesmaids. I clicked on their conversation and read as my husband apologized for spending so much time complaining about me. He referred to naked pictures they'd discussed on their most recent phone call. My stomach twisted and turned. My hands shook as I stared blankly at the words until they grew blurry through the cascade of tears. I didn't want to know if there was more. I slammed his laptop shut and waited for him to come home.

I'd hoped that a confrontation would elicit apologies and declarations of love, but instead, it seemed that the revelation of his secret allowed him to finally drop the mask he'd been wearing since our wedding day. Compliments and kind gestures, though they had always been rare, seemed to disappear completely. They were replaced with complaints and criticisms. I'd always known that our relationship wasn't perfect, but now I saw that it was worse than I ever would have imagined it could be. I clung to his assurance that they never acted on anything and that all of it was a desperate attempt to stroke his ego and see if any other women would want him. The only way to numb the pain was to create a hazy existence where I never allowed myself to think too hard about our reality. I was currently failing at my endeavor, so I returned to my goal of getting drunk enough to forget.

Unfortunately, the wine was having the reverse effect, and I was reminded of the Christmas gift we'd given her a few months after I read the emails. He said that he wanted his sister to visit, but his parents would never allow her to travel so far with just her boyfriend. So, she had to bring her. It was too far a drive to make alone. I tried to refuse him. I didn't want to pay for her to visit. I never wanted to see her again. He'd already embarrassed me when he told her to disregard the message I'd forced him to send about cutting communication. He started typing it as soon as the first was sent, while I was just a few feet away. He really did think I was an idiot. But it meant that she knew that I knew. And at Christmas, she learned that he cared more about her than he ever did for me. He tried saying that I had "won" because he'd married me, but I didn't feel much like a winner. I was forced to swallow my jealousy and bear the nauseating sight of the two of them laughing and joking with his sister while I tried not to let my internal death become apparent.

I needed another refill. I returned to the patio and held my glass close to my chest as a soft breeze swirled around me. I leaned back, put my feet up on the second chair, and let the dizziness of inebriation overtake me. I let my mind drift through a peaceful haze of nothingness when the recent memories of our sex life started playing out in my head. The threat of infidelity had made me desperate to keep him fully satiated. Sometimes his drinking made his attempts at making love rather twitchy and ineffective, but I learned how to act out a scene that made him feel like an incredible lover. It was better than the insults he would spew if I didn't appear to be enjoying myself. I started forcing myself to endure the positions he'd move us into that elicited pain. The way his eyes would scan my body as it reflexively recoiled and clenched made it clear that it was intentional. He liked having that power over me, so I did everything I could to make it through until he climaxed. I even found ways to submit to his request for acts that I had refused him for years. I usually offered myself for the most nauseating deeds in the afternoon before he left for work because it was the only time of day that he was sober, and I could ensure that it wouldn't take him long.

I stood up and shook my head to rid myself of the negativity swirling through my mind. This was my life, and I needed to make the best of it. There wasn't a way back. We were married. That meant forever. Sometimes I fantasized about packing up the car and driving the fourteen hours home in the middle of the night before he woke up, but what could I say when my family asked why I'd come home without him? I always made sure they thought I was happy. And it really wasn't that bad. So many people had far more difficult lives than I did. I was being ridiculous and feeling sorry for myself, and I was better than that.

I needed a mood shift, so I put on some music. It flowed through my ears and blocked out the doubts and the fears that had started surfacing. I held my drink in the air as I swayed and twirled and sang along. I let the familiar melodies and lyrics penetrate my heart and soothe the wounds that had started to burn. I drank, and I danced, and I let myself forget. I pushed away the intrusive thoughts that had overtaken my mind, which had grown weak with intoxication. I'd finally gotten to the point where I was drunk enough to smile and enjoy myself. I lost track of time, but when my clothes started growing damp with perspiration, I got another refill, retired to the couch, and turned on the TV.

I didn't know what time he'd be home, but I wanted to be awake when he got here. I wanted to embrace him and let myself believe that we were in love. I settled in to wait as I found one of my favorite shows playing a late-night marathon. I was a bit off balance on my next trip to the fridge, and the box of wine was getting lighter and needed to be tilted to fill my glass. When I sat back down, I stared at the screen, but I wasn't paying attention to the show. I started thinking about how my husband may be broken, but I understood his pain. I knew why he lashed out and why his insecurities often got the best of him. He needed me. I doubted that anyone else could love him the way that I did. He needed someone who asked for nothing from him and gave him kindness, patience, and warmth. I could do that. I swelled with pride at my noble purpose. I knew that if I just worked hard enough, eventually I could become the wife he'd always wanted.

My stomach started grumbling so I went to the kitchen for a snack when I realized that the sun had started peeking through the window. I couldn't believe how long I'd stayed up. I made myself a quick bite to eat and stumbled to the bedroom. When I woke up, he was lying next to me. I didn't want to disturb him, so I quietly made my way to the kitchen for some breakfast. A couple of hours later, he joined me.

"What time did you get home last night?" I asked.

He stretched and yawned. "I don't know, sometime after six, I think." He scratched his belly, opened the fridge, pulled out a forty-ounce bottle of malt liquor, and poured himself a glass. "Can I see the remote?" he asked before sinking into his recliner. I smiled as I passed it over and watched him as he flipped through the channels. I was glad that he'd had a fun night out. I wanted to ask him what they were up to for so long, but he would probably just get annoyed, so I left it alone.

His confession came a few months later.

"I slept with someone else."

My mind reeled as I tried to imagine who he could have slept with before we started dating when we were sixteen.

"I met her at the bar with my friends. She asked me for a ride home and then if I wanted to come in and watch TV. It just happened."

"Oh," I whispered. He meant recently. I sat and stared at the floor as the silence pulsed through the living room.

"You're not reacting like I thought you would," he said with his face twisted with confusion.

"Okay." What could I say? I'd learned long ago that any complaints would be met with contempt, so I offered none. He relaxed into the evening and started droning on about his desperation to decide whether or not to reenlist. All I could offer was indifference.

"What is your problem?" he asked, glaring at me with fiery eyes.

"You just told me you cheated on me. I'm not really in the mood to be sympathetic." I mumbled as I crossed my arms.

"Well how do you think that I feel?" he exclaimed.

"What?" I was genuinely confused by the question.

"I'm the one who has to live with the fact that I cheated on someone."

Bewildered, I scoffed and went to the bedroom. I fell into bed and curled up under the covers, wanting nothing more than to shut the entire world out, but my head was pounding. The walls I'd built to keep the darkness at bay crumbled and years' worth of tears and agony spilled out of me. I howled and sobbed, but I couldn't fully express the anguish that was wrenching my heart. I wanted him to comfort me. I wanted him to care. But I knew he never would, so I let out everything I'd been holding in until I was hollow, with only small tremors still vibrating through my exhausted body.

Once the dam had broken, it seemed that the haze that kept me complacent was lifting. I started doing things that weren't solely for the purpose of making him happy. I made a few friends at church, joined a book club, and started volunteering at a local food pantry. When he totaled our car, the insurance money was substantial, so I convinced him to buy two cheaper cars since he was growing tired of having to be dropped off at work when I needed to drive somewhere. I even found a way to finish the last two years of my degree online within five months. When he got kicked out of the military because his body had been so damaged by his drinking that he couldn't pass a physical fitness test, we moved back home and stayed with his parents. Before I knew what was happening, I'd gotten a job and was moving into a new apartment alone.

The divorce was quick and simple. We owned no property and had no children. It had taken years, but I finally saw him for what he truly was: nothing more than a culmination of cruel and hateful acts that were used to keep me subservient and quiet. Having spent over a decade in such a sinister role, I knew there was no way he could wash away the black stain on his heart. Perhaps the drunken haze in which he lived his life would quiet the demons that had led him astray, but I would never again offer him any kindness. I could not forgive the torture of my former existence, so I closed the door to the past and built myself a bridge to a better future.

38

The Pool Party

Joylyn Chai

1. EXT. EARLY EVENING. SUMMER. BACKYARD POOL.

The light from the setting sun reflects and sparkles on a backyard swimming pool. Water laps the edges of the pool; the sound is melodic. A sparkling silver, high-heeled shoe floats on the surface and bumps into a hot dog.

2. EXT. SUBURBAN STREET. SUMMER DAY.

The suburban neighbourhood is peaceful. Automatic sprinklers turn on and spray water in gentle arcs across manicured front lawns.

SUZIE WONG - An Asian, teenage girl wearing sunglasses, a cropped oversized t-shirt, Lycra biking shorts, worn-out dirty sneakers, and lace-edged tennis socks. She has a knapsack on her back. She's happily riding her bike and listening to a Walkman. Suzie turns up the volume, bops her head, and sings along to the music.

3. EXT. FRONT PORCH. THE JACOBS HOUSE.

Suzie rings the doorbell at the Jacobs house and waits. MR. JACOBS, a white, well-groomed, middle-aged man with perfectly coiffed hair and a dashing smile, opens the door. Mr. Jacobs is the father of Suzie's best friend, CAROLINE JACOBS. Sounds of a party can be heard in the background: kids yelling, splashing water, music playing.

MR. JACOBS

Suzanne! Suzie! The Suze-ster!

(Mr. Jacobs holds out a fist for a greeting. Suzie enthusiastically raises her fist.)

SUZIE

Hey, Mr. J.

(Mr. Jacobs and Suzie engage in a short "hand jive." Mr. Jacobs hugs Suzie affectionately. He doesn't notice Suzie slowly inhaling the cologne he's wearing. She closes her eyes. Mr. Jacobs grips one of Suzie's shoulders and pulls away. He straightens the waist of his pants and winks at Suzie. She winks back at him multiple times. Mr. Jacobs clears his throat. Suzie starts to walk away.)

MR. JACOBS

You can change upstairs, downstairs, wherever you want. You know your way around. *(clears his throat again and pats his hair down)* Don't forget the rules of the pool– *(Suzie turns back to face Mr. Jacobs.)*

MR. JACOBS and SUZIE

(in unison)

No pee, no poo, no shoes!

(Suzie repeats the little hand jive. Mr. Jacobs laughs nervously, adjusting the waist of his pants again.)

4. INT. THE JACOBS' HOUSE. LIVING ROOM.

The Jacobs' house is tastefully decorated, uncluttered, and modern. Suzie is alone in the living room. She catches sight of a painting of a young Asian woman lying in a chaise lounge. She studies the woman in the picture, moving her head close to it.

SUZIE

(whispering) Get up!

(The woman in the painting turns her head. Her face is deadpan.)

SUZIE

(unfazed) If you don't, you'll be stuck there. Forever.

(The woman in the picture continues to stare. The reflection of Suzie's face in the glass appears superimposed on the picture.)

SUZIE

O.K.*(shrugging one shoulder)*Maybe later.

(Suzie is about to walk away, but changes her mind and gestures with both hands, mouthing, "Get up!")

5. INT. THE JACOBS' HOUSE. POWDER ROOM.

Suzie washes her hands and dries them on a towel. Decorative soaps and bottles of cologne line the sink counter. She picks up the bottles of cologne, smelling each one until she finds the same scent that Mr. Jacobs is wearing. She sprays some of the cologne on her wrists, taking pleasure in the smell. Then she slips the bottle into her bag. From the bag, Suzie carefully takes out a pair of sparkling high heels.

SUZIE

(self-assuredly) Don't forget the rules. *(beat)* Of the pool.

(Confidently, she winks at herself in the mirror.)

6. INT. THE JACOBS' HOUSE. DEN.

With the high heels on, Suzie is leaving the bathroom, shutting off the light and closing the door, when she hears moaning coming from the den.

The door of the den is slightly ajar and the room is dark. The only light emitted is from a TV screen. Suzie gently pushes the door open.

Mr. Jacobs is sitting in the room with the curtains drawn. He's breathing heavily. Suzie glances at the TV and sees a tangle of naked bodies. A woman's face, the same as the one from the painting in the living room turns to look at Suzie. The woman is frowning. Suzie glances at Mr. Jacobs in confusion and disgust. Mr. Jacobs' eyes are glued to the screen; his upper body is rocking rhythmically back and forth.

MR. JACOBS

(without taking his eyes off the screen) Why don't you come n' join me? This part's nearly over.

(Mr. Jacobs pulls the zipper up on his pants.)

SUZIE

(panicked) I don't. I can't.

(Suzie closes the door quickly, but it accidentally slams. She jumps and hurries down the hall.)

7. EXT. THE JACOBS' BACKYARD POOL PARTY. SUNNY DAY.

Teenagers in summer and swimming attire reminiscent of the 1980s are in small groups around the backyard. They're talking, laughing, drinking cans of soda and munching on snacks.

Caroline, an attractive, white teenager, stands out in the crowd. She's wearing an expensive-looking, semi-formal dress. Caroline is perched on top of a picnic table chatting with a flock of friends around her.

Suzie, distressed, rushes over to the picnic table and grabs Caroline's hand. Caroline, laughing, jumps from the table. Caroline looks down at their feet. They have on the same shoes. Delighted to see Suzie, Caroline twirls her around and starts to swing dance with her. The party-goers cheer them on.

SUZIE

(*slightly horrified and whispering in Caroline's ear*) Carol, your dad–

(*Caroline locks arms with Suzie and leads her to dance in a 1960's "Frug" style.*)

CAROLINE

(*nonchalantly*) Don't even ask. We've heard from Mom twice. Dad thinks she's shacked up with some guy.

SUZIE

(*downplaying her shock*) Wow. Mrs. J.

CAROLINE

I hope I don't become so–

SUZIE

(impulsively) Secretive?

(Caroline is taken aback, then laughs bitterly. They stop dancing.)

CAROLINE

You're lucky. Your folks are still–

SUZIE

Under the same roof but never talk?

CAROLINE

It could be worse. Look at me.

(Caroline waves off any further conversation. Suzie plasters a smile on her face and squeezes her friend's hand.)

* * *

BEGIN FLASHBACK:

8. INT. SUZIE'S APARTMENT. DAY

SLOW MOTION.

Suzie's apartment is cluttered with papers, cheap mismatched furniture, and bare walls. A middle-aged Chinese man is watching television. A sandwich is served to him on a plate. He grabs the plate, clearly displeased with the food, and begins to yell in Hakka, a Chinese dialect. Suzie's face appears on the TV screen. Violently, the man throws the plate at the TV. As the plate heads towards the screen, Suzie's face turns away in fright. The sandwich flies apart; the plate hits the TV screen and smashes into pieces.

END FLASHBACK.

9. EXT. THE JACOBS' BACKYARD POOL PARTY. SUNNY DAY.

SUZIE

You're right. It's not so bad.

(*Suzie smiles weakly. Caroline rolls her eyes at her, jerks her hand away and begins dancing again.*)

10. INT. THE JACOBS' HOUSE. KITCHEN.

Mr. Jacobs is in the kitchen with an apron on, preparing sandwiches on trays to take outside. Several times, he nervously glances out the window where he sees Suzie talking to Caroline. He pats down his hair before he opens the window.

MR. JACOBS

(*shouting*) Caroline! Suzanne! Gimme a hand in here!

(*Caroline and Suzie look at him. Caroline puts her hands on her hips and sticks out her tongue. Suzie rubs her forehead, trying to cover her eyes with her hand. Mr. Jacobs sticks his tongue out at Suzie and gestures for them to come inside. He closes the window.*)

(*When Caroline and Suzie arrive in the kitchen, Mr. Jacobs scans the two of them head to toe and pauses at their shoes. He grins at Suzie and whistles.*

Unembarrassed, Caroline strikes a series of poses. Feeling self-conscious, Suzie keeps pulling her t-shirt down to cover herself.)

MR. JACOBS

(passing a tray of hot dogs to Caroline) OK, Miss Big Shot, take this tray out to the BBQ.

(Caroline holds it, waiting for Suzie. Mr. Jacobs quickly eyes Suzie.)

MR. JACOBS

(addressing Caroline) What are you waiting for? Outtcha ya get.

(Caroline kisses Mr. Jacobs on the cheek, blows a kiss at Suzie, and leaves the kitchen.)

MR. JACOBS

Grab those buns from the table, sweetheart.

(Suzie snatches up two bags of buns and is about to leave when Mr. Jacobs calls her back.)

MR. JACOBS

Suzanne, you know Mrs. Jacobs left a couple weeks ago.

SUZIE

Yeah, but Carol hasn't said much.

MR. JACOBS

It's been tough for her. So, don't say anything.

(Mr. Jacobs nods in the direction of the den. Suzie's face flushes. She looks down at the hot dog buns she's holding and is resolved to cooperate. Suzie looks squarely at Mr. Jacobs.)

SUZIE

(quietly but assuringly) O.K.

(Mr. Jacobs approaches Suzie and gently tucks a strand of her hair behind her ear. Suzie bristles, steps away from him, and shakes her head in disapproval.)

11. EXT. THE JACOBS BACKYARD.

Suzie walks out of the kitchen. Mr. Jacobs is right behind her holding the tray of sandwiches. Suzie steps out the door to the backyard when Mr. Jacobs grabs her behind and squeezes.

MR. JACOBS

(whispering) Say nothing.

* * *

BEGIN FLASHBACK:

12. INT. SUZIE'S APARTMENT. DAY.

Suzie's face is on the TV screen in her apartment. Then the television is turned off and the screen goes black.

* * *

SLOW MOTION:

A sandwich and plate are in mid-motion about to hit the glass of the TV screen.

END SLOW MOTION.

* * *

END FLASHBACK.

13. EXT. THE JACOBS BACKYARD.

Suzie is enraged. Blocking Mr. Jacobs, she slowly begins to spin and swing the bags of buns like nunchucks.

SUZIE

(*growling quietly*) Do not touch me.

(*With a brush of his free hand and a dismissive sigh, Mr. Jacobs tries to get past Suzie. She blocks him again.*)

SUZIE

(*explodes*) Touch me again and I'll tell everyone!

(*Caroline and the party-goers stop and stare at Suzie and Mr. Jacobs. Suzie, still spinning the bags of buns, tosses one of them to Caroline. Caroline doesn't catch the bag. Instead, it falls to the poolside. Caroline, affronted, gapes at Suzie. Suzie crouches lower to the ground, spinning her only bag of buns faster.*)

SUZIE

Mr. Jacobs, what are the rules of the pool?

(*Mr. Jacobs narrows his eyes as if to challenge Suzie. Caroline, in disbelief, clenches her fists..*)

MR. JACOBS and CAROLINE

(*matter-of-factly and in unison*) No pee. No poo. No shoes.

(*Suddenly, Suzie flips the tray of sandwiches Mr. Jacobs is holding. Mr. Jacobs is startled, stumbles backward, and falls to the ground on the grass. The sandwiches fly in the air. Caroline scrambles over to her father, trying to catch the sandwiches. Suzie bolts towards the pool, ripping open the bag of buns.*)

SUZIE

(*gleefully*) What about food? You forgot food!

(*Suzie hurls one bun after another into the air over the pool. One kid, who is in the pool, catches a bun and starts eating it. Some of the buns splash in the water. Suzie takes off her shoes and throws them into the air.*)

* * *

SLOW MOTION:

Suzie's shoes fly over the pool and land and float in the water. The party-goers cheer Suzie on. Mr. Jacobs is screaming at Suzie. Caroline takes off one shoe and throws it at Suzie. Suzie ducks and the shoe lands in the pool.

END SLOW MOTION.

* * *

Suzie dashes around the pool, picking up shoes and flip flops and tosses them into the pool. Mr. Jacobs, still on the ground, slides the empty sandwich tray toward Suzie, hoping to trip and stop her. Suzie easily hops over the tray and grabs a brightly coloured beach towel hanging from a chair. With one high heel on, Caroline chases Suzie. Caroline runs the opposite way around the pool and finally faces Suzie. Caroline is out of breath and glowering. Suzie raises her eyebrows as if to encourage Caroline to engage with her. Suzie holds the towel like a bullfighter's muleta. The party-goers freeze in tableaux. Caroline charges. Suzie throws the towel up and away from her.

* * *

SLOW MOTION:

The towel unfurls over the pool and lands on the water.

END SLOW MOTION.

* * *

The party-goers resume action, splashing in the pool, talking, eating, dancing. Mr. Jacobs grabs a skimmer net hanging from the wall of the house and is frantically using it to get the buns and shoes out of the pool. Caroline strides towards Suzie and grabs one of her wrists. Shaking, she squeezes Suzie, trying to hurt her. Suzie, inhaling deeply, is triumphant.

Caroline begins to sniff the air around Suzie and looks quizzically at her. Cocking her head to one side, she furrows her face and bends her head to smell Suzie's wrists. Caroline raises her head.

14. INT. THE JACOBS' HOUSE. LIVING ROOM.

Instead of Caroline's face, it is the Asian woman from the painting in the living room. She is standing and smiling widely at the camera. She has a hot dog bun in her hand and throws it at the camera, smashing the screen.

The End

About the Contibutors

Alan Hill has been writing for over twenty five years and is committed to the ongoing and never-ending learning that is the craft of poetry. His latest book - 'In the Blood' was published by Caitlin Press in 2022.

Alena Graedon's stories have been published in *The Paris Review, North American Review, Southern Indiana Review, Pleiades, Southern Humanities Review,* and the *VICE* fiction issue. Alena's novel, *The Word Exchange,* was a New York Times Book Review Editors' Choice and Paperback Row pick and selected as a best novel of 2014 by Kirkus, Electric Literature, and Tor. Alena twice received fellowships from MacDowell and Ucross and also received fellowships from Yaddo, Lighthouse Works, Jentel, Virginia Center for the Creative Arts, and The Vermont Studio Center. She received her BA from Brown and my MFA from Columbia and is an Associate Professor of English at Monmouth University. Alena lives in Brooklyn, NY with her husband.

Anthony Chatfield lives in Philadelphia with his family and recently completed his M.F.A. at Drexel University. His work has been published in Hare's Paw, Levitate, The 33rd, and Making Waves. You can find more information on his website at www.anthonychatfield.com.

Colleen S. Harris earned her MFA in Writing from Spalding University. A three-time Pushcart Prize nominee, her poetry collections include The Light Becomes Us (Main Street Rag, forthcoming), Babylon Songs (First Bite Press, forthcoming), These Terrible Sacraments (Bellowing Ark, 2010; Doubleback, 2019), The Kentucky Vein (Punkin House, 2011), God in My Throat: The Lilith Poems (Bellowing Ark, 2009), and chapbooks That Reckless Sound and Some Assembly Required (Pork Belly Press, 2014).

Colton Johnson is a student at the University of Central Oklahoma. He is currently enrolled in creative writing and hopes to build a promising future in writing screenplays and skits.

CS Crowe is three crows in a trench coat that gained sentience after eating a magic bean. He spends his days writing stories on a stolen laptop and trading human teeth for peanuts. A poet and storyteller from the Southeastern United States, he believes stories and poems are about the journey, not the destination, and he loves those stories that wander in the wilderness for forty years before finding their way to the promised land.

Cynthia Yatchman is a Seattle based artist and art instructor. She shows extensively in the Pacific Northwest. Past shows have included Seattle University, the Tacoma and Seattle Convention Centers and the Pacific Science Center. Her art is housed in numerous public and private collections.

Daniel Lewis is currently working on his bachelor's degree in creative writing and plans to pursue his doctorate. Fiction writing is his passion, but he loves exploring the abnormal and interesting in all forms of writing. He is always thinking about something strange, even when trying not to.

E. A. McCarthey is a graduate student at the University of Central Oklahoma pursuing an MA in Creative Writing. She was a runner-up in UCO's 2024 English Department Poetry Contest, and her work has previously appeared in *Beyond Queer Words*.

Elizabeth Rae Bullmer has been writing since the age of seven. Bullmer's work has appeared in *Pensive: A Global Journal of Spirituality and the Arts, MacQueen's Quinterly, Cloudbank, Sky Island Journal, Her Words, Anacapa Review,* and *The Awakenings Review.* Her most recent chapbook is *Skipping Stones on the River Styx.* She's a licensed massage and sound therapist, facilitates writing/healing workshops, serves on two community poetry boards and is the mother of two phenomenal humans, living with three fantastic felines in Kalamazoo.

Jacie Eubanks was raised in Sallisaw, Oklahoma, and is currently a creative writing student at the University of Central Oklahoma. When she isn't writing, she's watching movies and thinking about other worlds.

John Delaney served as a curator of historic maps at Princeton University Library. After retiring, John moved out to Port Townsend, WA, and has traveled widely, preferring remote, natural settings. Since that transition, he's published *Waypoints* (2017), a collection of place poems, *Twenty Questions* (2019), a chapbook, *Delicate Arch* (2022), poems and photographs of national parks and monuments, and *Galápagos* (2023), a collaborative chapbook of his son Andrew's photographs and his poems. Nile, a chapbook of poems and photographs about Egypt, appeared in May 2024.

John Pring is a poet and author based in the UK, where he is a Master's candidate at the University of Sussex. He has work published or upcoming in *POETICS, Santa Clara Review, The Passionfruit Review, B O D Y, Meniscus, Oroboro, The Talon Review,* and others.

Joylyn Chai's writing has appeared in *The Fiddlehead, The Ex-Puritan, Ricepaper,* and elsewhere. Most recently, "Not Wanted in the Garden," published in *The Cincinnati Review,* was selected as notable for The Best American Essays 2024. Published in *The Under Review,* "Gridiron and The High Seas," was nominated for a Pushcart Prize. Joylyn is Chinese-Jamaican Canadian and teaches ESL, English, and Indigenous, Inuit, and Métis Contemporary Voices to adult learners and newcomers on the traditional territories of Tkaronto/Toronto.

Lily Horn is a student at the University of Central Oklahoma studying general English. She grew up in a small town in rural Northwest Oklahoma and discovered a love for literature at a young age. This manifested into a desire to pursue a degree in English. After graduation, she plans to obtain a job working as an editor. Her dream job is to work as a copy editor for one of the Big Five publishing houses. She enjoys reading, writing, being in nature, baking, and spending time with friends. Her favorite genre is Science Fiction and Fantasy, her favorite author is Olivie Blake, and her favorite books are *Looking for Alaska* by John Green and *Alone with You in the Ether* by Olivie Blake.

Lindsay Thurman is an author and advocate in Louisville, KY. She was diagnosed with Pulmonary Arterial Hypertension, a rare and chronic lung disease when she was just 23. She was originally given less than a decade to live, inspiring her to leave an abusive marriage and start her career as a teacher. Now she is thriving after beginning a treatment plan that includes three medications that did not exist when she was first diagnosed in 2008. She enjoys running, yoga, spending time with her family, and is passionate about raising awareness of rare diseases and the subtleties of emotional abuse. You can read more from Lindsay at Lindsay-Thurman.com.

Lindsey Warren is a Delaware native. She earned her MFA from Cornell University, and her three collections (*Unfinished Child*; *Archangel & the Overlooked*; *Sentence, Forest*) are available from Spuyten Duyvil. She has had poem collages published in various journals, including (but not limited to) *Fugue, Miracle Monocle, The Rappahannock Review, and Action, Spectacle*. Lindsey's Substack "Wilmington is a Poem" chronicles her city-wide public poem collage project about her hometown. She lives in Arden, Delaware.

M. Russek was born in Cleveland, Ohio. Dr. Russek has worked as an IT specialist, wildlife director, and editor, and took part in the 2008 economic crisis. M. Russek has won various photography and art awards, and is also a poet, teacher, editor, and essayist.

Matthew Wallace is a creative writing major at the University of Central Oklahoma.

Maureen Sherbondy's work has appeared in *Litro, New York Quarterly, Southern Humanities Review*, and other journals. Maureen lives in Durham, NC. www.maureensherbondy.com.

Michael J. Galko is a scientist and poet who lives and works in Houston, TX. He was a 2019 Pushcart Award nominee, a finalist in the 2020 Naugatuck River Review narrative poetry contest, and a finalist in the 2022 Bellevue Literary Review poetry contest. In the past year, he has had poems published or accepted at *Stillwater Review, Cagibi, Eclectica, Clackamas Literary Journal, Cordite Poetry Review* (Australia), and *Tar River Poetry*, among other journals.

Robin (Echo) Young, based in Borrego Springs, has been working in mixed media since her 20s, focusing mostly on collage and contemporary art making. Her focus on collage art using magazine clippings, masking tape, wallpaper, jewelry, feathers, foil, etc., allows her to delve deep into the whimsical and intuitive compositions. From large, life-sized pieces and 3D sculptures to small postcard-sized arrangements, Robin's keen eye and gripping aesthetic guide her viewers into her own semi-ready-made world. Frequently re-purposing these nostalgic images for lighthearted and sometimes disquieting messages.

Rowan Waller graduated from Regis University with degrees in Psychology and English. Currently, she works as a rock climbing guide and outdoor educator outside of Durango, CO. Much of her writing discusses the psychological connections of humans to nature, and often dwells in memories of a tense childhood lived in the south. Her poetry has appeared previously in literary journals such as: *Owen Wister Review, The Palouse Review, Outrageous Fortune, Catfish Creek, The Albion Review, Nimrod International Journal, The Tulsa Voice, Panoplyzine,* and *Moon Shadow Sanctuary Press,* among others. Additional pieces are forthcoming in February editions of *Screen Door Review* and *Eunoia Review*.

Sara Shea received her BA from Kenyon College, where she served as Student Associate Editor for The Kenyon Review, and studied with David Foster Wallace. While studying abroad at Exeter University in the UK in 2000, Shea won a "New Millennium Poetry Contest" sponsored by The Queen of England, British Parliament, and judged by UK Poet Laureate Andrew Motion. Shea pursued graduate classes through UNCA's Smokey Mountain Writers Program and Western Carolina University, where she studied under Ron Rash. In 2013, her short story "Shine" won the grand prize for creative non-fiction through *Quarterly West*, and Shea was awarded a fellowship to Writers@Work. Her stories and poems have appeared in *The Connecticut River Review, Quarterly West, The Key West Love Poetry Anthology, Amsterdam Review, The Ledge, Wrath-Bearing Tree*, and *Petigru Review*. Shea writes professionally, producing marketing materials for a fine arts gallery in Asheville, NC, and crafting compelling SEO property descriptions for luxury homes worldwide.

Savannah Brooks earned her MFA in creative writing from Hamline University and works as a literary agent for KT Literary. Her work has been featured in the *Guardian, Hobart,* and *Every Writer's Resource*, among other publications, and has been nominated for a Best of the Net Award. A disabled writer suffering from the most literal of broken hearts, she lives in the mountains of Asheville, North Carolina, with her two black cats, Eggs Benedict and Toaster Strudel.

ZiXuan Angel Xin is a poet, essayist, and playwright based in New Jersey and Shanghai. When she isn't writing, she is probably sipping matcha.

To Order

Submission Information

New Plains Review accepts original work in poetry, prose, plays, and visual art. Submission information and editorial guidelines are accessible at newplainsreview.submittable.com.

***

Ordering Information

Pricing for issues is available through Amazon (search: New Plains Review and/or Shay Rahm).

www.ingramcontent.com/pod-product-compliance
Lightning Source LLC
LaVergne TN
LVHW021947060526
838200LV00043B/1950